The Messenger

Robin Valaitis Heflin

CUP

HARA
PUBLISHING GROUP

Published by
Hara Publishing
P.O. Box 19732
Seattle, WA 98109
(425) 775-7868

ISBN: 1-883697-12-3
Library of Congress Number: 99-071699

Manufactured in the United States
10 9 8 7 6 5 4 3 2

Editor: Vicki McCown
Cover Design: Bill Fletcher
Cover Photo: Lori Lovejoy
Desktop Publishing: Scott & Shirley Fisher

To Nana
I'll see you on the other side

Acknowledgements

Without the support of family and friends,
the writing of this novel would not
have been possible.
I offer my sincerest thanks and gratitude to:

My mom, who has supported my every
endeavor, this one being no exception... my
husband, Dennis, who kept me moving forward
when I might have given up and...
the Antelope Valley writer's group,
Karla Tipton, Margo McCall, Terri Shute, and
Helene Rauma, who offered encouragement as
they climbed their own mountains.

Prologue
1966

John Metcalf was six the first time he died and went to visit Grandma.

When John returned to his body, he found his father, Steve, forcing air into his lungs while his mother, Nydia, leaned over them moaning, "Oh, my God! My baby! My baby!" John opened his eyes, and his mother shoved his dad out of the way and grabbed him.

"Grandma says hi." His mother's shoulder muffled his words, but John knew he had to deliver the message from Grandma.

"Grandma says she's okay an' you don't need to worry about her. There were all these people with her. They knew me. I thought I didn't know them, but I did."

Over his head, his parents exchanged one of those meaningful looks. It was like hearing people speak in Spanish; he knew they were communicating, but he didn't understand.

"We discussed this." His father's gaze was level with his now. "Remember, Grandma died." His father's normally impatient tone contained an odd hesitancy.

"Like Peter," John answered, remembering his pet rabbit. He knew what death was. Death was when you went away and didn't come back. Unless of course, you were a bunny, and then you just went into a shoebox and were buried in the backyard.

"Just like Peter. Grandma isn't coming back."

"But I can visit her," John said.

"No, you can't."

"Yes, I can. I just pretend like I'm sleeping and then I go where Grandma went."

His father and mother conferred in a tight huddle, whispering as John waited in resignation. His grandmother had told him this would happen.

The huddle broke, and as he'd expected, his mother made him put on a jacket even though he wasn't cold and herded him and his twin sister, Sandy, into the car. His sister claimed his side, but John didn't care; he was too interested in his parents' whispered conversation in the front seat.

The words "he looked dead" and "he hasn't been the same since she passed away" filtered back to him.

At the hospital, he waited with his family in a big room with plastic seats and tattered magazines. His dad paced while his mother twirled a strand of hair round and round her finger.

Finally a nurse came out, called his name, and led him and his mother to a little room with a padded table and a lot of machines with TV screens. She took his temperature and left. They waited. His mom twirled her hair and didn't say anything.

A tap at the door preceded the entrance of a large man with graying hair. His head was bowed over a red tabbed file folder.

"I'm Dr. Weston." The man looked up from the chart and met Nydia's gaze. "Your son experienced an episode of unconsciousness?"

"I went to visit Grandma," John volunteered.

"My son stopped breathing. My husband gave him mouth-to-mouth resuscitation." Nydia twisted the strands of her hair into a tight rope.

"I went to visit Grandma," John contradicted her,

because she had it all wrong, and he'd been taught to tell the truth.

"This happened at his grandmother's house?" The doctor's eyes flicked to John.

His mother shook her head. "No. At home. My mother-in-law—Johnny's grandmother—passed away last year. Johnny's been having trouble accepting it. The . . . episode . . . happened this morning. Johnny was in his room." Her voice broke. "I found him on the floor."

"What did he look like when you found him?" Dr. Weston asked. "What was his color like?"

His mother shrugged. "Normal. He looked like he was sleeping. But when I shook him, he didn't wake up."

The doctor poked, prodded and tapped, then motioned to Nydia. The two stepped outside the room and shut the door. Minutes later, his mother returned alone. "They're going to run some tests," she said in answer to his questioning eyes.

A nurse stuck patches called electrodes to his head, and John got to watch lines that she said were brain waves blip across a TV. That didn't hurt. Then they took some blood. That did hurt, but he didn't cry. He watched the bright red liquid filling the plastic tube and thought of Grandma.

In the end, the doctor said he could find nothing wrong and sent him home.

Chapter One
1996

John Metcalf slammed on the brakes and slid his gray Ford Explorer into an available curbside parking space. "You lucky slob," he congratulated himself on his good fortune. He waited, watching in the side-view mirror for a break in the traffic stream, then jumped from the car.

As he drew abreast of The Pit Stop, a local watering hole, its door opened, spilling a man onto the sidewalk. Raucous music reminiscent of jet noise poured from the bar's dark interior, then faded to a dull throb as the door slid shut. John sidestepped the man as he staggered to his feet, hitched his pants more securely over broad hips, and lurched into the road to dodge traffic.

Through the barred, dirty windows of Al's Tattoo and Body Piercing Salon, the adjacent business, John could see Big Al putting the finishes touches on a dragon that curled down the side of a woman's neck. As Big Al looked up, John caught his eye and waved. Big Al returned the salute.

John continued on to his office, jogging up the narrow stairs wedged between the tattoo parlor and the vacant storefront next door.

Only the sign, a discreet navy blue and white shingle spelling the words *Spiritual Advisor* and promising *Confidential* services *By Appointment Only,* gave any indication of the business conducted within its walls. And that was the way John liked it.

He made every effort to create a low-key, businesslike atmosphere to overcome any residual reluctance clients might have in employing his services. His business depended on his image of credibility, so in its furnishings and décor, his three-room suite conveyed staid and respectable to the point of being boring.

A beige tweed sofa rested against one wall of the waiting room, flanked by parquet side tables upon which a variety of women's magazines were stacked. The taupe carpet underfoot was clean, if several years old. Soft track lights overhead banished the shadows from the room and illuminated tranquil landscape prints of Puget Sound that decorated the walls. Only a framed, calligraphied sign indicated the waiting room didn't belong in any one of a number of professional buildings.

Please Be Seated—I Know You're Here, it said.

After a quick visual inspection of his waiting room, John followed the short hallway into a slightly larger room containing a long table surrounded by padded high-backed chairs. The convergence chamber, as he thought of it. Off the far end of the chamber was his private office, guarded by another sign, reading *Employees Only*.

Here the real work occurred.

John double-checked his planner, reading the previous week's notes to prepare for his first appointment, Mrs. Montague Boswell. She kept up a running chess game with her late husband and used her standing Tuesday appointment to exchange chess moves.

She was one of his simpler cases. More complex was the case of Celine Dufresne, a new client, scheduled for an afternoon consultation. John knew little about her beyond what they'd discussed in a brief, but tearful, telephone conversation.

A recent widow, Celine was struggling to raise a young child alone and under financial hardship since the untimely death of her husband.

"Please, Mr. Metcalf, you must help me. I've tried everything else. You're my last hope," she'd begged, her voice breaking on a sob. "If I could only find my husband, my daughter would be set for life. I only want to help her."

"Are you sure that an attorney wouldn't be more appropriate, Mrs. Dufresne? I don't think there's anything I can do." John hated getting into the middle of squabbles over the assets of the departed, and he turned away many potential clients who sought him out because they thought he could do better than the probate court.

"Just let me see you in person. Then I can explain everything," she had said. "I'll pay you double your normal rate."

In the end, his curiosity overruled his wariness and he agreed to meet with her.

* * *

Delayed by a phone call, John barely had time to tuck in his shirt and smooth back his conservatively cut blond hair before the bell on the front door announced the arrival of Mrs. Boswell. She sat prim and proper on the edge of the sofa, her support-hose-covered legs crossed at the ankles, a foil-wrapped package resting on her lap.

She rose and extended her hand, knowing as few did these days that a gentleman did not shake a lady's hand unless it was offered to him.

John grasped her hand in a shake that was neither crushing nor wimpy. Too many people acted as if she would simply crumble into dust and ashes before them if they applied any pressure at all. Mrs. Boswell respected a firm handshake. She was old, not decrepit.

"I've baked you a strudel, young man." She handed him the package. "Prune."

"Thank you. But really, Mrs. Boswell, you didn't have to do that," John said, with utmost sincerity. He hated prunes. Mrs. Boswell frequently brought him baked goods; unfortunately, she seemed to favor shriveled plums.

"It makes me feel good to cook for man who appreciates a fine prune strudel as much as Mr. Boswell did," she said. The fact was, Mr. Metcalf held a warm place in her heart. Though he dressed a tad casually–she inventoried his khaki slacks, navy pullover, and brown deck shoes—he was never casual in his behavior. Unlike many young people, he didn't engage in excess familiarity and treated her with respect, always addressing her as Mrs. Boswell.

Although her given name was Clovis, since her marriage some 60 years before, she'd never used anything but her husband's name. Even Mr. Boswell, bless his departed soul, called her Missus. Things had started to go wrong with the world the minute everybody became Bonnie and Fred instead of miss and mister.

"You look especially lovely today," John said.

"Why, thank you." Mrs. Boswell couldn't help but preen slightly. Though the years had lined her face, gnarled her hands and slowed her walk, in her heart, she remained a pretty, sweet 16, the age she'd been when she'd met Montague Boswell. Though some of lady friends had allowed themselves to slide into ruin like antebellum Southern mansions, Mrs. Boswell took care to maintain her appearance with weekly trips to the beauty parlor and touch-ups on the blue tint. Today she'd donned a simple lavender suit, accessoried with a gold locket inlaid with a one carat diamond solitaire, a 50th wedding anniversary present from Mr. Boswell.

"Is there anything special today that you'd like to ask?" John stepped aside and allowed Mrs. Boswell to precede him into the conference room. Another sign of good manners. He really was such a nice young man. Just like the son she'd hoped to have. But, alas, she and Mr. Boswell had never been blessed with children.

"Just our game of chess," she answered. "I think I know what he's going to do, and I'm going to win."

She waited for John to catch up to her, and then leaned in close. "You could mention that Myrtle Waring divorced her husband and eloped with Joe Morris, Mr. Boswell's old fishing buddy. The two of them are acting like teenagers." Mrs. Boswell's voice lowered. "The police caught them together in the back seat of her car parked right outside his house! I mean, really! Why not just go inside?" Mrs. Boswell wasn't shocked, just practical.

John pulled out a chair and Mrs. Boswell gracefully lowered herself into the chair the way she'd learned years ago at Miss Winters Finishing School.

Familiar with the routine, Mrs. Boswell rested her arms on the table, palms open and up, and waited for John to round the table and take the opposite chair. Soon she'd be able to talk to Mr. Boswell. Oh, not directly, but the words John brought back would be his. A tear welled in Mrs. Boswell's eye and she blinked it back. She missed Mr. Boswell so much.

Life was a gift from the good Lord and not something to be wished away, but Mrs. Boswell would be lying if she said she feared death and did not look forward to being reunited with her husband. But, until then, she had John. John would help her.

John thought Mrs. Boswell appeared a little teary-eyed, so he gave her a moment to compose herself, taking his time dimming the lights before moving to the table. Once seated, he looked at her, noticing that the rod in her spine had stiffened again. He reached across the table and lightly covered her hands with his. "Ready?" She nodded.

John inhaled deeply and held his breath before exhaling in a slow hiss. He closed his eyes. Many clients like Mrs. Boswell closed theirs, while others kept them open, hoping to see perhaps an apparition flying around the room.

He took several more deep, slow breaths and then began to hum, a cross between a mantra and a chant. He told his clients the resonant nature of the hum created a universal vibration in the soul, whether of the earth or the netherworld. Afterwards, most clients reported that they had felt the vibration deep in their chests like the bass of loud rock music.

Although it was probably too dark to see his face, John flickered his eyes underneath his closed lids as if in REM sleep. Next he began to selectively tighten and release the muscles in his body, his shoulders, his thighs, his abdomen, his arms. He knew Mrs. Boswell would be able to feel the tension and relaxation.

Suddenly, he gave a deep shudder as if a shiver rippled down his spine. His head slumped to his chest and his hand went limp in Mrs. Boswell's. He could feel her hands tighten slightly around his as if to anchor his body to the physical world.

And John waited, forcing himself to remain still. He allowed his thoughts to meander, thinking of the upcoming dinner at his parents, Celine's visit, and the need to get the Explorer serviced. When he decided he'd been "gone" long enough, he collected his thoughts and began the process of rousing himself.

He twitched his fingers and then began to contract other muscles in his body at random. Slowly, John raised his head, blinking several times. He forced his vision to unfocus and looked around the room before bringing his gaze back to Mrs. Boswell.

"I left the message about Myrtle and Joe with the intermediary." John removed his hands from hers and flexed his fingers. "The message from Mr. Boswell is: 'rook to king's bishop two.'"

"I knew it! I've got him now. I can't wait to get home. I've got him checked." Mrs. Boswell clapped her hands. "What else did he have to say?"

"He says you should forget about investing your money in that annuity and should take a trip to Indonesia. He said the house looks really nice since you had it painted."

"He likes the blue trim?"

John nodded. "At first he wasn't so sure. He said initially he would have preferred gray, but the blue was a better choice."

"Did he say when I'd be able to join him?"

John shook his head. "It's not time. He misses you, though."

Mrs. Boswell's eyes filled with tears. "I miss him, too. It's not the same without him."

John reached over and clasped her hand. "You just hang on. It all works out in the end. Trust me."

Mrs. Boswell smiled through her tears. "You're such a nice man. I'm so glad Mr. Boswell found you." She undid the gold metallic clasp of her black patent leather pocketbook, removed an embroidered handkerchief, and dabbed at her eyes.

"This was part of my trousseau when I married Mr. Boswell in 1931." She slipped the handkerchief back in her purse. "I never used them much. Kleenex always seemed more practical. But after Mr. Boswell passed on, the handkerchiefs somehow made him seem closer to me." Her eyes sought reassurance. "Am I just a crazy old lady?"

"Mrs. Boswell, you're the sanest, smartest lady I've ever met," John answered.

* * *

"See you next week!" John waved to Mrs. Boswell as she drove away in her Lincoln Continental, then ascended the stairs and returned to his private office.

He checked that the answering machine was on, its volume off, and stretched out on the sofa, folding his arms on his chest. He closed his eyes and began to clear his mind.

The tick of the clock and the rush of the traffic faded until he heard only the blood rushing through his veins and the air whooshing from his lungs. His eyes rolled back into his head and his body went limp. One arm slipped off his chest and fell to the floor.

He could feel each beat of his heart as it struggled to pump blood through miles of vessels. His breathing labored. Inhaling took a long time; each releasing breath sent a shudder through his body. Each beat of his heart echoed in his ears.

Lub-dub, lub-dub, lub-dub.

Lub . . . dub.

Lub . . . . . . dub.

Lub.

Dub.

John took one last convulsive breath with his

final heartbeat. He rested in his body until the swirling atmosphere electrified, like the air before a thunderstorm, only more powerful. Then the passage yawned open, pulling him into a tunnel of light. He looked back, his gaze lingering on his recumbent form. Ahead of him, the light beckoned, and he rushed faster and faster toward the blazing brightness.

He passed through the decision zone where souls waited in Limbo, their last opportunity to make a U-turn and return to their bodies and lives. Snippets of their thoughts penetrated the fog.

Hey, that's me down there!

Wheee . . . I can fly.

Holy shit. Oops, sorry!

Time became elastic and unstructured. John focused his thoughts on the presence he wished to call. In a split second that could have been a lifetime, he emerged on the Other Side to find Mr. Boswell, a swirling ball of energy and motion, waiting impatiently.

"So she thinks she can win, huh? We'll see about that. I know what she's going to do. You tell her queen's bishop to king's rook two!" Mr. Boswell said not a word, but John heard the message.

Even after hundreds of trips to the Other Side, the sentience he acquired when he breached the barrier between life and death still awed him. He allowed himself a few moments to absorb the feeling before responding to Mr. Boswell.

In life, Mr. Boswell had been a crusty bantam rooster of a man who loved his wife with limitless affection, which had carried over to the Other Side. Two and a half years ago he and Mrs. Boswell had nearly been reunited when she'd suffered a heart attack. But the time hadn't been right, and unable to cross beyond Limbo, she'd been forced to return to her body. Before she returned, Mr. Boswell had told her she could use John to speak to him.

John fortified himself for the whirlwind that was Mr. Boswell and began to speak. "Your wife says Myrtle Waring divorced her husband and married—"

"Yeah, I know. Myrtle Waring never did have any sense, but she'll find that out soon enough. Tell Mrs. Boswell she'd better get her casserole dish back by next Tuesday because it's checkout time."

"I can't tell her that," John protested.

John's travel was bound by three conditions. The first stipulated he not reveal when people would pass on. The second said he could not interfere with the decisions of people in Limbo. Third, and most important, he had to rejoin his body within five minutes, or his physical brain, deprived of oxygen, would be irreparably damaged—if he managed to make it back at all.

"Tell her to go to Puget Sound Travel," Mr. Boswell said. "They're having a great package deal on tours of Indonesia and the Orient. She'll love it."

At once, the mist around Mr. Boswell grew melancholy. "We had always planned to travel around the world together when I retired." Mr. Boswell sighed. "We'd only just started when I passed on. A second doesn't go by that I don't miss her. I married her when I was too young and stupid to have the sense the Good Lord gave a turnip, but somehow I found Mrs. Boswell and married her. It was the best thing I ever did."

As instantaneously as remembered sorrow had infused the mist, it quivered with humor. "The only thing I don't miss is Mrs. Boswell's strudel."

John stared at him. "Mrs. Boswell says it's your favorite!"

Mr. Boswell snorted. "I hate prunes! When we first got married, Mrs. Boswell made me a prune strudel. I didn't want to hurt her feelings, so I said I loved it. That was the biggest mistake I ever made. "Take my advice. Don't lie to your young lady, John. It will only come back to bite you in the keyster."

"I don't have a young lady."

A grin lit the mist. "Yet," Mr. Boswell said smugly, faded into the vapor, and disappeared.

Tornado-like, the fog began to swirl, drawing John back into the tunnel as the blazing light diminished behind him. Ahead, he could see his body, supine and slightly blue, on the sofa.

John slipped into his body, the jolt of his spirit re-entering his corporeal self jump-starting his respiration and heartbeat. As blood coursed through his arteries and veins, his skin tingled, stabbed by hundreds of needle sticks.

From the sofa, John could see the message light blinking on his answering machine. Though his legs were heavy with numbness, John rolled to his feet and staggered to his desk. The machine beeped and whirled to the beginning of the tape.

"This is Celine Dufresne," came the frantic female voice. "I have to speak with you immediately. I know my appointment isn't until this afternoon, but if it's okay, I'm going to come early and maybe you can work me in."

And she'd hung up without leaving a number where he could reach her.

Chapter TWO

Not knowing quite when to expect Celine, John hung around the office making notes from the morning's session with Mrs. Boswell. Shortly before noon, the doorbell rang, and he went to meet his newest client.

His first impression was that she was trying to make one. Slim feet arched over spiked heels and curved into trim ankles that slid into shapely calves, stretching into firm thighs hugged by a black miniskirt. A lace camisole flashed beneath a short black jacket. Elaborately curled red hair framed her face, then drifted onto her shoulders. She noted his perusal with a small, knowing flash of a smile that seemed to belie her status as a grieving widow. As quickly as it appeared, the smile disappeared into a neutral, unreadable expression.

"Mr. Metcalf?" Her voice was husky, almost hesitant. "I'm so relieved you could meet with me on such short notice. You must be a very busy man with a lot of clients."

She was tall, her height nearly equaling his six feet, John noticed as he shook the hand she offered.

"I'm sorry I had to change my appointment, but something came up at work and I knew I wouldn't be able to get away later. This is very important to me and to my daughter's future financial security."

"That's no problem," he said. "I had an open slot, but in the future, it's probably best to keep your scheduled appointment or reschedule it if you can't make it. If

I'd been with another client, I wouldn't have been able to meet with you."

"You take your business very seriously," she said.

"I take my client service very seriously. Each of my clients is entitled to my undivided attention while we're in session."

"Have you been in business here long?" she asked. He watched as Celine's gaze panned the waiting room so slowly she almost seemed to be taking inventory of the furnishings.

"Several years," he answered. "Let's go into the conference room and do some preliminary work. I'd like to get some of the specifics about your situation."

John led Celine into the convergence chamber, where she selected a seat at the oak table, nearest the door. She crossed her legs, and placed her bag within quick reach on the table.

"I like to talk to my clients before beginning a session. I need to know a little about them, what they're looking for, why they came to see me." John studied her as he took the opposite chair. This close, a trace of dark roots showed through her auburn hair, and he decided the cornflower-blue color of her eyes probably came from tinted contact lenses.

Her head cocked slightly. "If you're psychic, shouldn't you know all that already?" she asked.

"If by psychic you mean someone who can predict the future, I'm not psychic. That's why I have a dialogue with my clients prior to any session, so we can clear up any misconceptions and achieve a common understanding and set of expectations."

"But don't you advertise yourself as a psychic?" Her eyebrows arched over a gaze so hawklike in intensity, John felt as if he were under surveillance.

"I don't advertise much at all. Most of my business comes from word of mouth. I'm a spiritual messenger. I act as an intermediary between the living and their departed loved ones."

"So you're a channeler?"

John shook his head. "No, that's not quite it. Spirits don't speak through me, nor do they possess my body and speak through my voice. I meet with the spirits, they give me the message and then I come back and relay that information to my client."

"Ah, that's where the messenger part comes in." She nodded in apparent understanding. "How long have you been doing this?"

"Over ten years," he answered, omitting that he'd been traveling to the Other Side since he was a child. Tension knotted between his shoulder blades. For a woman as frantic and tearful as she'd been, it didn't add up. She was more interested in his business than in telling her story.

"Do you really think you'll be able to speak to my husband, Quentin?" It was the first information she'd shared since she had arrived

"Whether I can speak to Quentin depends on the information you provide. I need to tap into the departed person's wavelength. The more information you can give me, the better chance I have of reaching the person. If I can't reach the intended person, there's no charge to the client."

"But I'm sure you reach nearly everybody." That small knowing smile reappeared.

"Actually, I don't," he denied. "Some people are simply unreachable." The fact was, people didn't want to receive bad news and had the tendency to figuratively shoot the messenger. John had learned early on to reveal only the good news and step around the bad.

"How quickly can you get an answer?" Celine asked.

"What's the question?"

"I need to contact my husband, Quentin Black." Celine leaned forward on her elbows. Determination lit her eyes with intensity. "Our daughter, Ashley, is six months old. Quentin has never seen her. He died before she was born."

Celine paused, as if trying to select the right words. "Quentin and I, we weren't married, yet. We were planning on it, but it always seemed like we had plenty of time. He told me he had set up a trust fund for Ashley. But then he died.

"Now his ex-wife claims she has his will and that it leaves everything to her. Quentin wouldn't do that to his daughter! I just know it. There must be another place, a safe deposit box or something."

It was on the tip of John's tongue to tell her that her sort-of husband might have done exactly that, but he held back the words. Instead, he asked, "When did he die?"

"A month before Ashley was born. I was away—visiting my mother—when someone broke into the house," Celine stopped. She looked down at her lap. When she raised her head, a veneer of tears glistened in her eyes. "They killed him. I came home and—and—and I found him!"

She fished in her bag, pulled out a Kleenex and blotted her eyes. "I know that Quentin is gone, but I'd like Ashley to be cared for the way he would have wanted."

John knew with absolute certainty she was lying.

Whoever she was, she hadn't come because of a daughter's trust fund. It wasn't just that her story sounded like a network Movie of the Week; something about her raised the hackles on the back of his neck.

"I think I can help you," he said.

"You can?" Droplets of faux tears glinted off spiked lashes. She reached for her handbag. "Do I pay you now?"

John raised a hand. "No, you pay me after services are rendered. I'll bill you. Let's set up a session for next week, say Wednesday at two o'clock, and we'll get to work."

* * *

If John's house had been a blind date, he would have been described it as having a good personality. Nothing in the compact two story with mismatched paint, missing shingles and a touch of dry rot could be called attractive, but it had what John required—a garage and a basement.

As he entered the house, he was met by Stanley, one hundred pounds of eager, boisterous doggy-smelling fur and slurping tongue.

"Okay, that's enough." John wrestled with the dog for a moment, then not-so-gently—because Stanley was not one to understand subtle hints—pushed him aside.

John peered out the window for the neighbor's cat, and not seeing it—let Stanley out for a run. Stanley was a notorious cat chaser, although he'd never actually caught one. Still, neighbors didn't appreciate seeing their cats flee in mortal fear.

With Stanley's needs filled, John's thoughts

returned to Celine. He'd never had such a strong feeling of unease about a client before. What was she after? His rational side told him to reject the case, but his impulsive side urged him to accept the challenge. When he evaluated his work objectively, he had to admit that exchanging chess moves and neighborhood gossip wasn't all that fascinating.

Still, prudence bade him to check out her story.

John changed into a comfortable pair of old sweatpants and T-shirt and stretched out on his bed. Slowly, he began to clear his mind. The room faded away as his consciousness called to the light. The tunnel opening appeared and he was pulled from his body, floating toward the brightness.

"Johnny!" His grandmother enveloped him in a hug. Neither she nor John had physical form, yet the sensation of being touched was still there.

"I hear you're having dinner at the folks," she said. "Tell Stephen and Nydia I said hello." She chuckled in amusement.

"Right," he answered sarcastically. "You know what happened the last time I did that. Ever since, Dad has thought I'm nuts."

"He's my son and I love him, but if I didn't know better, I'd swear he was somebody else's child. He has no imagination, no sense of adventure."

"Not like me." John filled in her unspoken words.

"Not like you," she repeated.

"I don't feel very adventurous. I want what everybody else wants. A good marriage. Two point three children. A house in the suburbs. Two dogs and a cat."

His grandmother shook his head. "You want those things, yes. But there's more to you than that. Look at

you. Would you be here if you were just Mr. Jo‸
age? You've always taken chances, danced with d‸
Would you be considering taking Celine Dufresne ‸ ‸
client if you didn't?"

"Speaking of which, what can you tell me
about her?"

"Just that she doesn't have a daughter, Quentin
Black doesn't exist and never did."

It was pretty much what he'd suspected. "Who is
she then? What is she after?"

"She's a special investigator with the vice squad
of the Seattle P.D." She allowed her words to soak in,
then she laughed. "You're under investigation!"

"What did I do?" John didn't see the humor.

"They think you're conducting a scam to bilk little
old ladies out of their retirement funds and young widows out of their life insurance."

"Why would they think that?" John conducted his
business honestly and discreetly. Most of his clients
were referred to him by other satisfied customers. What
could he have done to attract the attention of the
police department?

"Remember Candy?"

John winced. He did remember Candy. Forty-
something housewife. Fight with husband before
business trip. Husband dies of a heart attack while on
business trip. Candy wants to tell husband that she's sorry.

Only John found out it hadn't been the stress of
the husband's out-of-town meeting that did him in, but
the extracurricular sexual calisthenics in his hotel room.
Because he'd felt Candy needed the closure, he'd broken
his own rule about relaying bad news and told her the
truth. She'd appeared to take the news well at the time,
but he'd evidently misread her.

"The police shined it on at first. But Candy's neighbor married a city councilman and the rest is history," his grandmother explained.

"He put pressure on the police department." John sighed. "Why didn't you tell me this sooner?"

"John, you know I can't reveal things that change the choices you make. I'm skating on the edge as it is."

"At least tell me something about Celine that I can use."

"Her dad's a cop. Her brother's in the military. Her mom is a dispatcher with the police department. She's been with the P.D. for five years, since she graduated from the academy. She's well connected. Knows a lot of people. A lot of people. In fact, you and she may know some of the same people. That's all I can tell you."

Chapter Three

"How's Elvis?" Steve Metcalf slapped John on the back and guffawed at his own joke as John and Sandy arrived for dinner at their parents' house.

John shot his dad a censuring look, but Steve shrugged it off. "What's the matter, boy, can't you take a joke?" Steve turned from his son and greeted his daughter. "Hi, honey." He kissed Sandy's cheek.

"Dad, don't start, okay?" she responded. Sandy had often played mediator between father and son.

"Start what?" Steve's widened eyes feigned innocence.

Several other not-so-funny jokes followed before a temporary cease-fire was enacted for dinner. The meal passed peaceably, with everyone but Steve content with a generous first helping.

"Pass the pot roast, please," Steve Metcalf ordered, and reached for his belt buckle.

John waited until his father undid the button on his fly before handing him the platter of meat. He and Sandy exchanged a knowing glance. Steve Metcalf wasn't one to let discomfort prohibit him from going for seconds. Or thirds, for that matter.

"Where's Reid tonight?" John asked his sister. Her husband was an attorney for a smoke detector manufacturer.

"On a business trip." She sighed. "He's been traveling a lot these days. We hardly see each other anymore."

"And you say my grandchildren are spending the whole week with Reid's folks?" Nydia's tight-lipped expression made it evident that sit well with her. She and Reid's mom competed for time spent with the grandkids. Sandy never lacked a babysitter, but keeping both sets of grandparents happy was an impossible task.

Sandy simply nodded, hoping to avoid the subject. John recognized the look on his sister's face. Dinner with the folks was field of land mine subjects to be avoided.

"I hardly ever get to see them," Nydia complained.

Sandy rolled her eyes. "You had them last week, Mom."

"Was it only last week? It seems longer. It wouldn't be so bad, if I had other grandchildren." She aimed a pointed stare at John.

"Say the word, and I'll get right to work on it," John said. "Of course, I can't promise you'll also get a daughter-in-law."

"John! What kind of talk is that?" she chided. "I just want you to be happy. To meet a nice girl and settle down."

"I'd be happy if he got a real job. Put that college degree we paid for to work," Steve added grumpily.

John shook his head, looking first at his mother then his father. "Why do you have to do this everytime I come over? Mom, you nag about the grandchildren and Dad, you criticize my work."

"What are you talking about? I'm sitting here, minding my own business, trying to enjoy the meal your mother prepared. Pass the mashed potatoes. *Please.*"

John stared at him.

Steve's eyebrows rose. "Well? Are you gonna pass me the potatoes or what?"

"Here." John placed the dish a little harder than necessary next to his father's plate.

"You know, I never expected you to take over the plumbing business when I retired. I didn't want you to. Rooting around in people's toilets is no joyride and it's hard on the knees and back. And you always seem to get called out during the Super Bowl.

"I know, Dad," John started to interrupt.

"Let me finish. You have a college education. Both of you." His glance included Sandy, a criminal defense attorney.

"You have opportunities your mother and I never had." Steve sighed. "I just don't understand."

Before John could reply, his mother cut in. "What's happening with that big case you're working on?" she asked Sandy.

"You know I can't say anything. Confidentiality." Across the table, his sister fiddled with her silverware, avoiding their mother's eyes. John wished she would say something to keep the conversation from focusing on him. Fortunately, his mother wasn't so easily deterred from her interrogation.

"You go to trial Monday, right?" Nydia didn't wait for an answer. "I read about it in the paper. That big developer, George Larkspur came home and shot his wife as she was sleeping. What kind of man would do such a horrible thing?"

"It hasn't been proven that he shot his wife. Larkspur says intruders killed her," his dad spoke up.

"*The World Examiner*—"

"Is a piece of garbage," his father finished for her.

John's mother was unfazed. "I think it's wonderful that our daughter is working on such a famous case. The paper even printed her picture."

"If anyone's picture should be in *The World Examiner*, it should be John's," his father said. "'Psychic Discovers Aliens Living in the Space Needle.'"

"I think I'm done." John stood up and tossed his napkin on the table. "It was a great dinner, Mom. Thanks. I'm gonna get some air."

"What about dessert?" she protested.

"I'll have some later, maybe." He left the room.

"I was just kidding!" his dad yelled after him.

John made his way to the front porch and found the swing in the dark. He rocked slowly, staring at the star-studded sky. His sister had given him a lift so he couldn't go. He had no choice but to wait.

He knew his father meant well. But like so many other people, Steve's vision was limited by convention. It was beyond his capability to understand things that weren't tangible, things he couldn't see with his eyes or feel with his hands. Leaky toilets, stopped drains, that's what his father understood.

That his son could communicate with people who'd died wasn't something Steve believed was possible. He'd never believed it. Not even the moment it had first occurred.

After that first trip to visit his grandmother, John had talked non-stop about the Other Side. "When I die, I'm gonna go live with Grandma on the Other Side. We all are," six-year-old John had said. "It's really neat there. There aren't any toys, but it's still fun."

His father had told him he didn't want to hear any more about it, and later, John had heard his parents talking, their voices audible through the thin, tract-house walls. His father was angry.

"I don't know what's wrong with him," his dad said.

"The doctor said he's all right," his mother had answered in a hushed tone.

"He's not all right. All this talk about Mom. Like he still visits her. He knows she dead! He went to the funeral, for Christ's sake! It's weird. It gives me the willies."

"It's probably just a phase . . ."

"God, I hope so." Steve's response had been fervent.

"We can take him to see a child psychologist . . ."

"No!"

"There's nothing wrong with that. Jennifer down the street took her daughter."

"Jennifer's daughter bangs her head against the wall." Steve paused. "It's not like he doesn't have any friends. He hangs out with the other kids. What's that one who keeps coming over here, the one that always has snot running down his nose?"

"Jerry."

"That's the one. And Sandy's John's age. She's his twin! If he didn't have friends I might be able to understand him making up an imaginary playmate."

"John and your mother were so close."

"But she's *dead*. He knows that. He has to."

"I know." John didn't realize he'd spoken aloud until he heard his sister.

"Who are you talking to?" The screen door slammed, and Sandy moved to the swing.

"Just myself," he said. "I always hope it will be different, but it never is." He sighed. "I'm surprised you came tonight. I thought you would have gone with Reid." Although busy with her work, Sandy joined her husband on his business trips whenever she could.

"Reid and I decided it would be best if he went alone."

Something in her voice made John look at her. "Everything okay?" he asked.

"Yeah. Yeah. Nothing serious. We just haven't been getting along well lately. We decided that this trip might give us a little breathing space."

"I'm sorry to hear things aren't going well."

"Don't worry about it," she said. "I'm not. We've just hit one of those rough patches every marriage goes through."

"Well, if you ever need to talk, I'm here," John said, hoping she wouldn't.

"Thank you."

Somewhere, a dog howled. Crickets chirped nearby. A gentle breeze rustled the trees that dotted the front yard and filled the air with a subtle pine scent. The street lamp had died, casting the house and its environs into the dark. The stars of the northern sky were clearly visible.

"You're not seeing anybody," his sister said.

"No," he said with resignation.

"I thought you and Cindy . . ."

"I may talk to dead people," John said. "But Cindy was weird. She kept snakes."

The swing creaked as they rocked back and forth.

"So she had snakes." Her tone said, "You're too picky."

"So how'd you like to be . . . you know . . . in the act and have a boa constrictor wrap itself around your ankles. It really spoils the mood."

Sandy laughed.

"I'm not kidding."

"Have you met anyone else? I know a woman at my gym . . ."

"No more. What is it about married people that they can't stand to see someone alone and happy?"

"That's fine as long as you are happy."

"I'm . . . content."

"But not happy."

"I didn't say that," he denied.

"You didn't say you were."

"I just don't want you to fix me up with anybody. I'm sorry I went along with it the last time. But, actually, I have met someone. She's very interested in me."

"That's great!"

"Her name is Celine Dufresne. She's got long legs, a mass of red hair and a great set of—"

"John!"

"Handcuffs." He grinned.

"I don't want to hear it."

"She's a police officer."

"You're seeing a cop?"

"I'm being _investigated_ by a cop," he corrected. "She thinks I'm trying to con little old ladies out of their life savings. She's posing as a client."

"Do you need help? I know a good lawyer who'll give her brother a great deal."

John shook his head. "Thanks for the offer, but I can handle it."

"John," Sandy started, then hesitated. "Don't take this the wrong way, but have you ever considered a different line of work? You do have a degree in business."

"Now you sound like Dad. '_Et tu Brute?_'"

"That's not fair."

"Isn't it?" John looked at her.

"Maybe Dad's not all wrong." The edge that had

crept into her voice softened. "I know you believe in what you're doing. But couldn't you believe in something else?"

"It isn't what I believe in, it's what you and Dad and Mom don't believe in. I'm so damn tired of having to defend myself all the time. You know, I could have hid it all. I could have pretended to have a nine-to-five job. I could have let you all believe I'm a midlevel manager for Boeing or some other large corporation, but I didn't. For my honesty and openness, I've become the butt of jokes and the disappointment of the family."

"I'm sorry. You're my brother and I love you."

"But you think I'm a wacko." John sighed. "I don't want to fight. I just want someone who trusts me, who believes in me. That's obviously not you, so let's drop the subject."

From inside the house came the blaring noise of bells ringing, a signal that _News Flash_, a TV expose show, had begun. His dad, so disdainful of the tabloids his wife read, believed every word he heard on _News Flash_.

John caught his sister's eye. "Dad's waiting for the day when you appear on _News Flash_ to discuss some high profile mass murder case you're working on."

"God forbid." Sandy shuddered. "Are you ready to go?"

"More than ready."

They rose and went into the house to say their goodbyes.

"Don't you want dessert? I have ice cream—two flavors and chocolate syrup. You can make a sundae," Nydia protested when they announced they were leaving.

"No, Mom, thanks. I'm full," John said. "Thanks for dinner. It was great."

"You outdid yourself tonight." Sandy kissed her.

Steve sprawled in the recliner, a soup dish of vanilla ice cream with fudge topping resting on his abdomen. His eyes were glued to the television.

"We're leaving, Dad," John said.

Steve turned his attention from the TV. "Don't run off."

"Sandy has an early morning," John lied.

Steve balanced the dish of ice cream on the arm of the recliner and struggled to his feet. "Hey, John, you know I was just giving you a hard time. Don't let it bother you, okay?"

His dad always apologized, but John knew the next time he saw him, it would be the same old thing again.

"Yeah, I know. I'll see you around," John said.

Chapter
Four

John sprawled on his tan leather sofa, feet propped on the low coffee table. Since arriving home, he hadn't bothered to turn on the lights.

The sounds of night crept out of the darkness and he wanted to enjoy them: the hum of distant traffic, the song of the crickets, the creaking in the old house, the ticking of the kitchen clock.

He figured it was near midnight. Through the open drapes, the night sky was filled with thousands of stars, little specks of light that revealed the insignificance of human existence and then some, because the human eye could detect only a fraction of the number of stars. In reality, there were billions, trillions, quadrillions, perhaps an infinite number of stars.

Of course, he thought wryly, he didn't need the stars to remind him of his insignificance. That's what his father was for. He was thirty-six years old and self-supporting. So why did he still continue to chase his father's approval?

Too tired to answer the question, he began to unfocus his mind, allowing his consciousness to wander. His respiration and heart rate slowed, stopped, and he slipped over to the Other Side.

He had no person to see, he just needed to get away. Recharge. Rethink. The mist swirled around him, filling him with peace. He felt centered, at one with himself instead of torn in different directions.

He allowed himself to float, absorbing the sensation. Time passed. A millennium—a second—he wasn't sure which, although somewhere in his earthly consciousness a biological clock ticked. Gradually, a presence made itself known. A woman. From her he felt not peace, but sorrow and indecision. He realized he had floated into Limbo.

He was going to leave her be, but her words called out to him.

I can't go back.

Who are you? he asked.

I must go back, came the confusing reply.

Who are you? Why can't you go back? He could feel her foundering.

I'm Heather. Pause. *I'm dead, aren't I?*

Not yet. You have a choice. John reached out.

I think I killed him.

Who? he asked. And suddenly he knew.

I shot him. He wouldn't stop! He wouldn't stop! Oh My God . . . He's dead.

He's not dead. John tried to calm her, stem her panic. *If he were dead, he'd be here, too.*

Haltingly: *Then . . . I'm dead?*

Not yet. But you must choose. You can continue on to the Other Side or you can return.

I can undo everything that has happened?

Not even God can do that. But you can see the choices that led you to where you are and take a different path from here on.

The veracity of his words had their impact on him as well. He needed to go forward, to take another path. For too long, he'd been coasting through life.

Are you an angel? Heather asked.

I'm just a messenger. John smiled.

What will happen to me?

That's for you to decide.

Her thoughts broke away from him and she faded into the mist. He felt a momentary emptiness at the separation and then became one with himself again. She was gone.

John drifted, cleansed by a void of thought. For a long time, his soul floated, seeking no one. After a while, he felt another presence calling to him. He focused his consciousness and found his grandmother waiting.

"You almost crossed the line, Johnny," she admonished. "Not everyone in Limbo has a choice. But some do and they must make their own decisions. You're not supposed to influence them."

"I only told her she *had* a choice. She seemed so lost."

"I know it's difficult. But it has to be that way. If people have free choice, they must be free to make their choices and not be influenced by someone who has greater insight, knowledge and power. By coming to the Other Side, you have the greater ability to See. To Know. You must not use that power to influence."

"I know," John answered, feeling uncomfortable, not at his grandmother's chastisement, but at something else. Something was wrong. What?

"Just be careful you don't break the rules. There would be serious repercussions if you did."

The rules! Time was one of the rules. "How long have I been here?!" John gasped. Although time was elastic on the Other Side, it marched along linearly on Earth. If he didn't return to his body within five minutes, he could suffer brain damage, become "locked in," unable to travel.

"I have to go!" John pulled his thoughts away and tried to free his mind. What time was it? What if he was too late? Concentrate. Concentrate, he told him himself. His soul floated in the mist, like debris caught in the undertow of a river, and he struggled to focus. He was unable to call up an image of his bodily form. Snippets of the thoughts of the souls around him filtered to him, disturbing his concentration.

"How will my children get along without me, they're so little."

"Have you met the Big Guy yet?"

"Wait until they find out I left all my money to the Home for Aged Cats."

A diversion. He needed a diversion, something to focus on. The mist! With supreme effort, he forced the conversations out of his mind and began to think of the mist. Mist swirling around him, blanketing his mind, protecting him, comforting him. The mist that drew him here and took him back. Gradually, John's mind cleared and then he focused on his body. He visualized himself sprawled on the sofa, a still, lifeless form. His head had fallen to one side.

The tug toward life began, and John was propelled from the Other Side, slowly at first, then with greater speed. The tunnel opened and John was drawn back to earth and into his body.

He woke up gasping. Violently, he sucked the air into his lungs, struggling to replenish the oxygen. His chest heaved with the effort. Exhausted, he felt as if he'd run a marathon.

He knew he had almost died. Permanently.

* * *

John checked out the window for the neighbor's cat, saw that the coast was clear, and let Stanley out to get the newspaper. The dog bounded out to the driveway, reappearing moments later with the weighty Sunday *Seattle Times*.

He gave Stanley a few of the doggy biscuit treats he favored, then carried the paper upstairs to his bedroom, where he's left a cup of coffee on the bedside table. He looked forward all week to the-Sunday-morning-coffee-and newspaper-in-bed ritual.

After he scanned the headlines and read a few of the top news stories, a small wire story on page twenty-four caught his eye. An Iowa woman had shot her husband, then locked herself in the car, engine running. A neighbor noticed exhaust seeping from underneath the garage door and called the fire department.

The woman was later arrested in the shooting, but claimed self-defense. John closed his eyes and said a silent prayer for the woman he had briefly met on the Other Side.

John took his time perusing the paper, saving the most amusing section for last: the personals. He got himself another cup of coffee and began to read.

Female rocker into heavy metal, body piercing and civil disobedience seeks artistic but macho guy for good times. I'm 5´8, platinum blonde and shapely. You should be tall and handsome. CPAs, engineers need not apply.

Love is a contact sport. Women's rugby champion seeks adventurous athletic male for the game of love. I like hockey, football, rugby, soccer, and bullfighting.

And my family thinks I'm weird, John thought. But the next ad stopped him short.

Stargazer. Single female who likes to dream seeks companion for life's journey. I am 5´6, attractive, blond, green-eyed. I like long talks, good books, walks in the woods, old movies and picnics.

For a moment, John considered the possibilities. He'd never responded to a personal ad before. He imagined meeting the woman. Blond. Green eyes. Long legs, shapely. His mind completed the details not covered in the ad.

Then his mind filled in the probable reality: Overbleached blond hair. Makeup applied with a trowel. And more pounds per square inch than a baby killer whale.

He shuddered and tossed aside the newspaper.

John jumped out of bed and pulled on a new pair of gym shorts and his favorite T-shirt. The formerly white shirt was now gray and ripped in places, but it matched his sneakers, which were equally gray and dingy.

He called for Stanley and on the way out the door, dumped the newspaper in the recycling bin. A gentle breeze blew from the north, chilling his bare legs, but John knew he'd warm up after he'd been jogging for a while. Stanley loped along beside him, easily keeping up with the undemanding pace, occasionally stopping to anoint a tree or hydrant.

Once around the boundaries that marked his neighborhood—the old Victorian mansion that looked haunted, the mom & pop grocery, the huge oak tree on the corner of Sycamore Street and Elm—equaled about a mile and a half. John tried to run at least three times a week and was up to four and half miles.

His sneakered feet pounded the sidewalk, and the sound resonated in his ears. *One. Two. Three. Four.*

One. Two. Three. Four. John counted to the beat.

Soon the wind ceased to feel cold, and sweat beaded on his forehead. His T-shirt clung to his chest, plastered to his skin by perspiration. After three times around the neighborhood, John decided to increase his distance, and it was on his fourth circle that he saw her.

She matched the kind of woman the personal ad purported to describe. A mass of shiny blond hair softly framed a face composed of delicate features. Her build was slim but attractively shaped with the nicely defined leg muscles of a runner. Sporting a red sweatshirt, neat white walking shorts, and spotless tennis shoes she looked as if she could have stepped from the pages of sportwear catalog.

The perfect woman, if it weren't for the yappy lap dog of some pedigreed origin attached to the leash around her wrist. But nobody was perfect.

Engrossed in the fantasy, John ignored the low sound Stanley emitted until the dog took off.

And then John spotted the cat. It was following the woman with the dog.

"Stanley, no!" John shouted.

The cat screeched and sprinted for the nearest tree. The little lap dog barked excitedly and tried to follow but only succeeded in tangling itself around the woman's legs.

"Suki!" the woman screamed, whether at the cat or dog, John wasn't sure.

The cat reached the tree a split second before

Stanley, who snapped at the cat's retreating tail. The cat disappeared into the branches, hissing and spitting somewhere among the leaves. The woman untangled herself and made it to the tree as Stanley began to bark in loud woofs. The little dog joined in, yapping, its body jumping up and down with each squeak.

John rushed to retrieve his dog.

The woman turned on him. "Do you see what you did?" she yelled, her delicate features now stern, accusing. "Call off your dog!"

It was what he'd been planning to do, but it annoyed him that she issued orders like a drill sergeant, reining in green recruits.

"Stanley, come on," John called.

The dog ignored him, continuing to bark and circle the tree, trailed by the squeaking ball of fur.

"Stanley, heel boy!"

"Don't you have a leash?" The woman snapped, grabbing the cord dangling from her dog. "Missy, stop it!" She yanked at the leash.

"Stanley doesn't like the leash. He usually follows right beside me." John grabbed the dog by the scruff of the neck and yanked him away from the tree.

"Well, he didn't this time, did he!" the woman snapped.

From inside the branches, the cat yowled in such a pitifully painful, one would have thought the dog had actually captured it.

"Seattle does have a leash law, you know!" The woman fired at him before turning her face up to the canopy of leaves. "Come on, Suki. It's okay," she spoke soothingly to the cat.

Attractive or not, the woman had an attitude. Okay,

his dog had chased her cat up a tree. But that's what dogs did. It wasn't like it was the end of the world.

"So why isn't your cat on a leash? And who takes a cat for a walk anyway?" John shot back while keeping a grip on Stanley, who was trembling in repressed excitement.

"Your dog is a vicious menace." She glared at the quivering Stanley.

"At least he *is* a dog! He's not some useless, yappy hairball that your cat coughed up!"

"Oh, aren't you the witty one! Why don't you take your dog and go home?"

"Why don't you?" John responded. It occurred to him that they'd reverted to the level of second grade one-up-manship. *My dad is bigger than your dad.*

"Because your dog chased my cat up a tree!" And following her comment came a plaintive wail from the treed Suki.

To that, he could think of nothing to say. She was right, and it irked him. So, keeping a grip on Stanley's neck, he led the recalcitrant dog away as the woman continued to call her cat.

John rounded the corner and, out of sight of the woman and her pets, released Stanley. Who in the world takes a cat for a walk anyway? he fumed. She had to know that sooner or later something like that would happen. Stanley wasn't the only cat-chasing canine in Seattle.

Of course, he should have leashed Stanley, given that he knew the dog's predilections. "No more free-range roaming for you, boy," he told the dog.

By the time John got home, he'd begun to regret his behavior. Yes, the woman had an attitude, but wouldn't he have acted the same? Her cat shouldn't have been out on the street, but his dog should have been under control.

And he hadn't even stayed to help her. The cat would probably hide in the tree all day.

John let Stanley into the house and then returned to the tree. When he got there, the woman and her pets were gone.

* * *

It was miracle that Suki had come down. Karyn Walker had feared that her cat would remain in the tree for hours. But after the man and his beast of a dog were out of sight, Suki had crept down the tree.

And now that they were home, the cat acted like nothing had happened. Missy, however, told another a story. The dog was in a whirl, refusing to settle down. Because of Karyn's irregular and long hours at the hospital where she worked as a medical social worker, Missy spent a lot of time alone. Karyn had taken the dog for a walk to release some of her pent up energy, but the excitement had had the opposite effect.

And the guy hadn't even stayed to help her get Suki out of the tree. Okay, Karyn reluctantly admitted to herself, she _had_ told the guy to go away, and he couldn't very well get the cat out of the tree with his dog still there, and in the end Suki came down on her own accord.

But still.

And his nerve! It had been his dog that caused the problem, and rather than being apologetic, he'd insulted her dog, calling little Missy a hairball!

Karyn watched as the quivering little dog raced around the house like a fuzzy wind-up toy and began to laugh.

Chapter Five

John raised his head and shook himself as if he'd been jolted awake from a deep sleep. Across the conference table, Mrs. Boswell peered at him.

"Queen's bishop to king's rook two!" he relayed Mr. Boswell's message from a week ago.

"That's a really odd move," she said. "I think Mr. Boswell is losing his touch."

John suppressed a smile. Wouldn't Mr. Boswell love hearing that? He was probably stomping around, fuming and swearing. He considered himself quite a chess player, although John thought Mrs. Boswell had the edge. She'd won three of the last five games. Mr. Boswell had accused him of not delivering the messages correctly, even though they both knew that wasn't true.

"Mr. Boswell advises that you get your casserole dish back from Mrs. Waring. He's concerned about it," John said matter-of-factly.

"Myrtle Waring has never failed to return anything she's borrowed." Mrs. Boswell straightened in the chair.

"I'm just relaying the message," John said.

"Message acknowledged," she said.

"He also suggested Puget Sound Travel would be the place to go to arrange the trip to Indonesia."

"I always use Scarborough Travel," Mrs. Boswell said in a haughty voice. She was argumentative today.

"He seemed to think Puget Sound Travel would give you a good deal."

"I will take it under advisement." She stood up to leave. "I'll see you next week. The same time."

* * *

Today, Celine wore a form-fitting red dress with three-quarter length sleeves and a gold chain belt that cinched her waist. She had twisted her red hair into a sleek French knot, except for a few a tendrils which, by design or accident, slipped free to frame her face.

He still had no specific plan on what to do with Celine, but one thing he had decided was to have a little fun. He wasn't concerned about antagonizing an officer of the law; he hadn't done anything illegal. If Celine wanted to waste her time snooping around, he'd go along.

"I think I have a good chance of locating Quentin," he greeted Celine in a smooth, confident voice.

An ersatz expression of gratitude filled Celine's face. "I'm so glad. The trust fund would really secure my daughter's future." Seemingly eager, she entered the conference room and took a chair, again by the door.

He took the opposite chair and wondered if she were wired, and if so, where under the form-fitting dress she could hide the microphone. Maybe it was in her bag.

"How much do I owe you for this session?" she reached for the suspicious purse.

John waved his hand. "My basic rate is fifty dollars an hour, but you don't pay until I achieve results."

"You guarantee results?" she cocked an eyebrow.

"I can't guarantee anything," he said. "It's out of my hands. I do guarantee to do the best job I can, spirits willing. But, you'll have an answer today," he answered.

"What do I need to do?"

John shook his head. "Nothing. You've taken the

first step by coming here. I only need you to tell me specifically what you'd like Quentin to tell you."

"I want to know where Quentin's latest will is. Tell him Ashley and I love him and miss him."

John reached across the table. "We need to hold hands," he explained. "It helps to strengthen the link to the spirit world."

Her expression blank, Celine grasped his hand.

John shut his eyes and, taking his time, followed the deliberate process of humming, breathing, contracting his muscles, shuddering. He could feel her eyes upon him, studiously observing every nuance. The hairs on the back of his neck tingled under her scrutiny.

He remained motionless, his breathing as shallow as he could make it.

He waited until he felt Celine begin to get antsy and then he waited some more.

Finally, he shuddered violently.

Celine jumped.

John's body convulsed, not with fake contractions, but silent laughter. Slowly, he flexed his muscles. First the fingers on one hand, then the other. Then his arms, shoulders, thighs.

He lifted his head and opened his eyes, staring straight at Celine's face. For a moment he said nothing, letting Celine wonder perhaps if he were in a trance.

"The spirits have told me that there is a missing link. I do not have all the information I need. There must be something more you could tell me," he said.

Her hands twitched, and she pulled them free of his. "I don't know anymore than what I've told you." Her eyes were wide, innocent, but her nostrils flared.

"I can't find any trace of Quentin Black." John shook his head as if puzzled.

"I don't see how that could be," she insisted.
"Maybe you didn't go into your trance deep enough.
Maybe you should try again."

"Are you sure you've told me everything? I must
have complete information."

"I think so. His middle name is Kendall, if that
helps. It's very important that I find the trust fund," she
insisted and dropped the tidbit that was supposed to be
the coup-de-grace. "Quentin had told me it would be
around $750,000."

"Three-quarters of a million?" John feigned interest. "Perhaps I'd better try again."

"Thank you."

He squeezed his eyes shut tight and began to chant
louder. He could feel his mouth twitching. He wanted to
laugh. Instead, he convulsed and then went still. His head
slumped to his chest.

He stayed "out" for ten minutes. Celine was barely
able to contain her impatience. Though her hands were
still, John could feel the vibrations from the tap of her
foot against the floor. It made him even more determined
to maintain the charade as long as he could.

At last he lifted his head and opened his eyes.
Again, he remained silent for maximum effect.

He stared into her blue-tinted eyes and freed his
hands from hers. "He's not there."

"What do you mean, he's not there?" Celine's
brows drew together, and she pushed back slightly from
the table.

"What do you think I mean?" John folded his arms
against his chest.

"How would *I* know what you mean? You're
the psychic!"

"In the first place, as I explained during our

consultation last week, I am a messenger, not a psychic. Secondly, I can't bring messages from people who never existed, dead or alive."

"W-What do you mean?" Celine stumbled slightly, then recovered.

"You made up Quentin Black. You're not a widow with a daughter—you're an undercover police officer with Seattle P.D."

"That's preposterous!" Celine blustered. "What would make you say such a thing?" She leaped to her feet. "You know, I really thought you'd be able to help me. But I can see that you can't." She inched toward the door.

John pushed his chair away from the table, and she backed up through the opening.

The bell on the front door signaled a visitor had entered the waiting room. A moment later, a man's voice drifted back to them. "Hello? Is anyone here?"

"The cavalry?" John asked dryly.

Without another word, Celine fled to the waiting area. John followed and found a thirty-something man with a conservative haircut, wearing an equally nondescript gray suit. An altogether forgettable character.

A plainclothes detective.

"Could you tell me how to get to the highway?" he asked and stepped between John and Celine, who gave him a little nod and then left.

"If you think it's up here, you're really lost," John answered.

John could hear Celine's heel clattering down the stairs, and the man decided he didn't need the help after all. "You're right," he said. "Sorry for bothering you." From the window, John watched Celine and the man climb in a beige van and drive away.

John exhaled. His heart raced, and a thread of perspiration trickled down his temples. He'd been more nervous than he'd realized.

* * *

Karyn answered the door to find her best friend hidden behind a bulging mailbag.

"Hi! Sorry I'm late. I had some reports to fill out and then I had to stop at the post office." Her friend breezed in and dropped the bag on the sofa where it bounced twice, tumbled to the floor, and spilled its contents.

Letters. Hundreds of them.

"What's all this? Did you rob the post office?" Karyn joked.

Celine Dufresne laughed. "This is what's going to turn your life around. No more sitting at home, waiting for Mr. Wonderful, girl."

"Celine, it scares me when you talk like that." Karyn's smile fled as her stomach gave a small clench. "Aren't we going to grab a bite and a show?"

"Later. Let's open your mail." Celine tucked her hair behind her ears and pushed up the long sleeves of her sweater.

The fist of unease twisted tighter. Karyn stared at her friend. "Celine, what have you done?"

Celine was the first person to befriend Karyn when she'd moved to Seattle. When her fiancé Drew broke off their engagement, Celine, like a mother hen, had taken Karyn under her wing, made her laugh, and nagged her into continuing with her social life when Karyn would have withdrawn. In retrospect, Karyn realized it was exactly what she had needed to keep her from dwelling on her loss.

Karyn had often admired Celine's take-charge style, but sometimes Celine overstepped the line. Karyn suspected this was one of those times.

"I put an ad in the paper," Celine answered serenely, her expression all innocence.

"What kind of an ad?" Karyn's voice was sharp.

"A personals ad. These letters are from men who want to meet you." Celine took a seat on the sofa as if it were an ordinary day and she hadn't done anything unusual.

"Please tell me you're kidding." Karyn grabbed a handful of envelopes. They were addressed to someone named Stargazer. "Stargazer?"

"That's the tagline that you used in the ad," Celine explained.

"That *I* used in the ad?"

"Don't get excited," Celine said in a calm voice, similar to that of a 911 operator calming a hysterical caller. "I thought it was time for you to start dating again."

"*You* thought?"

Celine ignored the accusation. "This is a great way to meet men. You'll have hundreds to choose from. Tall ones. Professional ones. Rich ones. Tall, professional, rich ones."

"Not to mention mama's boys, the chronically unemployed, and the psychos. As a cop, you should know better. And it's not your place to decide what's right for me. Did it ever occur to you to ask me what I wanted?" Karyn realized she was still holding the letters and tossed them on the sofa in disgust.

"Don't get your panties in wad. This is a great screening device," Celine countered. "You write to the guy. Talk to him on the phone, get a little info, and I'll run him through the computer at work. When he passes, you can make a date in some neutral, well-lighted territory."

"No."

"When was the last time you had a date?"

"That's none of your business."

Celine regarded her steadily, a hint of pity flickering in her eyes. "You spend every Saturday night alone." Celine was one of those women to whom men were attracted like moths to a porch light. Celine probably hadn't spent more than two Saturday nights alone since junior high.

"I do not!" Karyn felt her face flush at the lie.

"When was the last time you had a date?"

"Not long ago."

"Not since Drew, I bet."

"That's not true. I've had plenty of dates since then." *Two dates.* One with a forty-year-old editorial assistant who still lived with his mother, and the other with a man who'd interspersed "you know" into sentences so many times Karyn thought she'd go mad.

Celine regarded the mulish expression on Karyn's face and obviously decided that the best course of action would be to retreat a little. "Okay, I'm sorry," Celine said. "You're right. I was wrong. I overstepped the bounds of friendship and good taste—"

"—Again." This wasn't the first time Celine had exceeded her authority, but it was, by far, the most egregious incident.

"Again," Celine conceded. "But the deed has been done, so why not take advantage of it?" With a fiendish glee, she tore open a letter.

Karyn stared in disbelief. "You're reading my mail! That's a federal offense!"

"You don't want it!"

"That's not the point." Karyn snatched the letter

out of Celine's hand. "Give me that!" She scanned the letter, then dropped it, almost as if it were dirty. "This is almost pornographic!"

"Let me see." Celine perused the letter. "I don't know. It's a little kinky but . . . Oh look, he enclosed a picture. He's . . . sort of attractive." She held up a photograph of a naked tattooed man astride a Harley.

"Your taste in men leaves something to be desired." Karyn began scooping the mail into the bag. Bag in hand, she marched to the front door.

"Where are you going?" Celine asked.

"To the trash."

"Don't do that. Karyn . . . the guy has a Harley!"

Karyn shot her a withering look.

"Okay, that first one was a little crass, but I'm sure there's at least a few good ones in there."

"No. Celine, You've been a very good friend to me, but don't ever do this again."

With satisfaction, Karyn shoved the bag of letters into the garbage. She wasn't so desperate that she would resort to a personal ad to get a man.

Chapter Six

Big mistake.

Nothing else could quite describe what he'd done. What in the world had possessed him?

John made rings on his paper napkin with the bottom of his coffee cup. The cup was empty, his waitress was on break, and her fill-in was unconcerned with tables that weren't hers. But he didn't need any more coffee. He was wired enough as it was.

For the umpteenth time, he glanced at his watch. Five minutes to eight. It was still early. Still time for her show. Still time for him to sneak out.

Please, God, let Stargazer be a normal person, John prayed, his mind reviewing previous dating debacles. The nonstop talker, the woman trolling for a rich husband, the militant feminist who'd given him a ten-minute lecture when he'd opened the door for her. His waitress returned from break and refilled his cup. He told her there'd be two of them and he'd wait to order until the other half of his party arrived.

Party hah!

There was no party. Only one very big mistake.

Somewhere between the time he'd returned from jogging and the return of his senses, he'd pulled the newspaper from the trash and answered Stargazer's ad.

Her name was Karyn Walker. That knew because she'd called him on the phone and they'd spoken. For some reason, she'd sounded familiar to him and from that fragile base, a budding rapport had grown. But they were both cautious, so they'd agreed to see each other on grounds that it wasn't a date, but a no-obligation meeting.

So why was he so nervous about a meeting?

He watched as the door to the diner opened and an older couple entered, then a lone woman.

His stomach plunged at the sight of her.

It couldn't be *her.*

She spotted him a split second later.

Surprise and recognition flooded her face.

She glanced back at the door and John wondered if she was considering making a run for it. Instead, she slowly approached the table. John stood up. She was dressed as casually as he, only on her, jeans looked much better. The neck of her loose-knit sweater slipped down to reveal the round of her shoulder.

"John?" The color had receded from her face.

"Catwoman!" He burst out. "I mean, you're the woman with the cat. Sucky or something."

"Suki," she corrected.

"I thought you sounded familiar on the phone," he said weakly.

"You, too." She slid into the booth.

John took his seat. The napkin he'd been playing with looked rumpled and shredded, visible evidence of his nerves. "This is a surprise," he said, and mentally cursed his triteness.

"I certainly didn't expect to see you here," she agreed.

"I, uh, went back to find you. To help you get your cat. But you weren't there. I'm really sorry about what happened." John started to fiddle with his napkin, caught himself and forced his hands to be still.

"Once your dog left, Suki came down," Karyn explained. "I'm sorry about the way I acted. It was probably only a matter of time before something like that happened."

She was gracious in admitting her culpability in the incident, John noted. "I'm glad Suck—*Suki* wasn't hurt. Stanley chases cats when he can, but he's never actually gotten one." He pushed a menu across the table. "I waited to order until you arrived."

"I'm not hungry. I'll just have a cup of tea."

John flagged down the waitress and Karyn placed her order.

"In your ad, you called yourself a stargazer," John ventured.

She laughed, slightly self-consciously. "A friend of mine made up that name for me. It's kind of silly. I just enjoy watching the stars. The night is so peaceful and quiet. Other-worldly."

"Are you into astronomy at all?"

She shook her head. "No. You?"

"No. I guess that's something we have in common. We share a lack of interest in astronomy," he joked. "I did take an astronomy class in college. Astronomy is a lot about measuring light, distance and wavelength. Somehow, thinking of stars as huge, fusing balls of gas takes all the fun out of it." He'd actually taken a lot of science classes in his quest to learn more about the physical world and how it differed the Other Side.

What he learned was that while much was still a mystery about the physical world, it could be defined and described. There were no words to describe the Other Side.

"Astrology?" John smiled.

Karen shook her head. "I don't even know what

my sign is. I'm too much of a pragmatist to go for that kind of hocus-pocus."

The waitress delivered her tea. As Karen squeezed lemon into it, she said, "So, John, what do you do?" Her head was bowed over her task so she didn't see his involuntary start.

He'd known the question would arise, and berated himself for not having an answer ready. He needed to tread lightly, test the waters. He couldn't just blurt it out. *I'm a messenger boy for dead people. But enough about me, how about you?*

One thing he knew for certain—the truth would be the quick end to what he hoped would be a promising date.

"John?" Karyn was looking at him now. "I asked what you do for a living."

"I, uh...help people communicate with...each other," John said, carefully stepping between truth and fiction. "I'm a communications consultant."

"Like a communications facilitator?"

"That's a good way to put it," he said.

"Do you work for a large corporation or a small firm?"

"I have my own business. It's a one-man show," John said. That was true, anyway.

"And you work with corporations?"

"Mostly individuals. One-on-one training."

"That sounds great. I know some of the doctors at the hospital I work at could use communication training. They've gotten better, but some of them have no idea how to talk to people or to how to translate medical jargon into layman's language so patients and their families can understand."

"You're a nurse?"

"A medical social worker. At Seattle Hospital. I help to connect patients and their families with hospital and social services that can help them. I'm kind of a patient/family member advocate." She took a sip of her tea.

"So you have a degree in social work?" John asked.

She nodded. "UCLA. You?"

"Business. University of Washington. I'm glad I got it, but if I had it to do over again, I'd major in something that applied more to what I do."

"A degree in business doesn't help you in running your own business?" Karyn asked, a frown crossing her face.

Damn it. That was the problem with lying, you really had to pay attention to what you said. "I mean, I do use it, somewhat. But all the stuff about management when you're a one-man show doesn't really apply," he improvised. "I should have studied communications. You said you went to UCLA. Did you go to school out of state, or does that mean you're not a Washington native?"

"I've been here for about two years. I came with my fiancé. He got a job as an engineer at Boeing. I followed him here, but when I arrived, he decided he didn't want to be married."

"I'm sorry."

"I'm not. His loss." She shrugged.

Well." John cleared his throat. He picked up the unused fork and studied the tines. The silence stretched for an interminable moment and then they both began to speak at once.

"You—" he said.

"First—" she said.

"You first," he said.

"First dates can be really awkward." She smiled and sipped her tea.

He nodded vigorously. "I hate first dates. Except of course for this one," he corrected himself. What was it about a date that made a person get stupid?

"Of course."

"But then this isn't a date. It's a meeting."

"That's what we agreed."

A crash of shattering dishes and a muffled curse drew his attention to the kitchen. John glanced at the swinging door then back at Karyn. "You must have gotten a lot of responses to your ad."

"A couple hundred letters."

"And you picked me. I'm honored."

"You seemed normal."

"Your glowing assessment of my character warms my heart," he said without rancor. He had been dating for half his life and knew exactly what she meant. Hadn't his fervent wish been that she would be normal? "Placing an ad in the personals seems kind of risky for a woman, though."

Something very interesting seemed to be at the bottom of her cup. He hoped she was reading the tea leaves. That would be a good sign. Her chin lifted, and she met his eyes.

"I didn't place the ad."

"You didn't?" His eyebrows rose.

She shook her head. The light from the overhead hanging lamp caught the highlights in her hair and made it gleam.

"My best friend did. I didn't know anything about it until she showed up at my house with all the letters."

John chuckled. "I'll bet you were furious."

"Furious doesn't even come close." Karyn

grinned. "I read the first one and threw the rest away."

"The first one being mine."

> *Dear Stargazer,*
> *I'm sure you will get a lot of letters promising the stars. I can't give away what isn't mine. I'm just an ordinary guy who likes dogs, children, old movies, jogging and tennis. I can give you a bit of myself and perhaps a trip to the moon every now and then.*
> *Sincerely, John.*

His letter must have sounded pretty good. Self-confidence surged through him.

"No." She shook her head. "That first letter pretty much scared me off."

"Then how?"

"I found your letter under the sofa a week later when I was vacuuming. Curiosity got the better of me."

"So I suppose your friend is gloating that her trick worked."

"She would, and that's why I didn't tell her. But I've forgiven her. What about you? Do you often answer personal ads?"

"My first one," John said. "I read them for fun. Some of them are pretty scary. But yours caught my eye. Writing to you was an impulse thing, which I immediately regretted."

The instant the words left his mouth, John realized what he'd said, "I mean—"

Karyn smiled. "No offense taken. I know what you mean."

"Thank you. You're very understanding," he said

and realized she was. She no longer blamed him for her cat's harrowing experience, she'd forgiven her friend for her transgression, and she took it in stride when he said stupid things. Furthermore, she was in a profession where she had to be nonjudgmental. Surely that boded well?

"More coffee? Hot water?" The waitress checked back and John realized most of the people in the coffee shop had left.

"It's getting late," Karyn said, reading his thoughts.

"I guess we'd better let them go home. I'll walk you to your car."

John nabbed the check and left the waitress an extra large tip since they'd tied up her table for several hours. He paid the tab while Karyn waited.

Slowly they walked to their cars. John hooked his thumbs into the pockets of his jeans, as he strolled beside Karyn. "I don't think our pre-date went too badly."

"No. I enjoyed meeting you. Both times." Laughter lurked in her voice.

"Do you think we're ready to advance from a meeting to a date?" John felt his mouth go dry and his stomach do the cha-cha. It was hard to get the words out.

She looked up at him. "I'd like that."

He felt relief and elation sweep over him. "Next weekend?"

"Great." Her teeth flashed.

"Sunday? How about a picnic? I'll bring the food and a bottle of wine."

"Okay, since you're bringing the food, how about if I drive?" she asked.

"Let me give you my address," John patted his pocketless sweater.

"Do you have a business card?" she asked.

He did, but he couldn't give her a card that read,

John Metcalf, Spiritual Advisor. "I didn't bring any tonight." Obviously, if he pursued this relationship—and he was sure he wanted to—he was going to have to tell her the truth soon. But this wasn't the time or the place.

"Here use mine." She extracted a card from her purse, and John wrote his address on the back.

He escorted her to her car, a little red Mazda Miata, parked under a street light. They shook hands, and then John watched as she drove off.

Chapter
Seven

Into the picnic basket he'd received from his sister for Christmas, John loaded the lunch: fried chicken, potato salad, marinated mushrooms, fresh fruit, French bread. Beside him, Stanley sat at attention, hoping for a handout. John ignored him and retrieved a bottle of chardonnay from the refrigerator. Stanley howled and shot John a pathetic look.

John shook his head. "No way, man. Not after you almost blew it for me by chasing her cat."

The doorbell rang, sending a musical tune throughout the house, startling him. It was too early for Karyn.

The beveled windows alongside the front door revealed his sister, Sandy, with children in tow. Dressed for a day on the go with the kids, she wore a pair of sweatpants and a baggy T-shirt, her hair pulled into a ponytail. Clutching one hand was Justin, his jeans and Ninja Turtle T-shirt bearing the stains of breakfast and an active morning. Hanging on the other hand was Chelsea in a ruffled pink dress, lace-edged socks and black patent-leather shoes. At three years old, Chelsea was already firm about what she liked to wear, and that usually included ruffles, bows or lace.

"Are you busy?" Sandy asked tentatively.

"Nah, I can entertain a *Sports Illustrated* swimsuit model anytime," John said, noting her eyes appeared a little red.

She followed him into the kitchen. "I *am* interrupting something." She eyes alighted on the picnic basket. "You have a date." She smiled smugly.

"What's that stupid grin for?"

"The picnic basket was a good idea, wasn't it?" she gloated.

John had thought the picnic basket was a silly gift, and promptly stowed it on the closet shelf, never figuring he'd use it.

"You were right. This once," he capitulated to end further discussion on the topic.

"Anybody I know?" Sandy fished, surveying the contents of the basket with interest.

"No."

"How'd you meet her?"

"Walking the dog."

"I told you dogs were a great way to meet girls. Women love men with dogs. It says they're great with children."

"If the children have four legs and eat dog food, I'd agree." John picked up Chelsea who'd approached him, arms raised. John gave her a loud smack on the cheek. She returned the kiss and he balanced her against one hip.

"Didn't you feed my son dogfood once?"

John flushed. When Justin was a toddler, John had briefly turned his back only to find that both Stanley and Justin were eating out of the dog's dish.

"Can I go outside?" Justin peered up at him, his arm tightly hugging Stanley's neck as the dog's tongue licked his face.

"Sure, sport!" John said, mussing Justin's hair. "But go easy on Stanley. He's just a puppy."

Justin giggled. "No, he's not."

Justin raced to the kitchen door and tugged it open.

Without waiting for an invitation, Stanley bounded outside. Justin followed, slamming the door so hard that the windows rattled.

"Down," Chelsea ordered.

John released her and she toddled to door. He let her out. "Justin—watch your sister," he called, knowing that his yard was fenced and kidproofed.

"So, what's up?" John pulled out a chair and straddled it.

"Nothing much. Tell me about your date."

John shrugged. "What's to tell?"

"Everything. What's her name? What does she do? Have you been seeing her long? Is she attractive?"

"Karyn. Medical social worker. No. And yes, very."

"Do you like her?"

"Would I be going out with her if I didn't?"

"What do you like about her?"

"Why don't I put on some pajamas, order pizza and we'll have a slumber party?"

"Don't be a smart-ass!" Sandy chided.

"I guess I don't see what all the interest is in my personal life. You and Mom act like I'm teenager and this is my first date."

"Maybe I'm a little envious," she said wistfully.

He stared at his sister. "Why? You're the one with the happy marriage, the wonderful kids, the great career."

She shook her head. "Reid and I never do anything like this anymore." Her gaze swept over the open picnic basket. "We used to have such fun together."

"Sandy, you're married. You have companionship, security. It's a different lifestyle than being single."

"I thought I'd have more balance. Excitement and security."

"Sandy, I'd trade what I have for what you have in a heartbeat. Do you know how many dates I've had with women I have nothing in common with? How many nights I've spent in front of the TV? I'm a thirty-six-year-old bachelor. Rather than seeing me as desirable, women are starting to wonder what's wrong with me. It isn't exciting anymore. I doubt it ever was. Now, tell me something positive about your life," John suggested.

"I just won a big case."

"Larkspur?"

"That's the one. My boss is thrilled. I got a big raise. There will be a write-up in the paper for mom to add to her scrapbook." Her voice was flat.

"I thought it would be exciting to run on the fast track, have a high-powered career and all. But it's not like that. It's demanding, and while there are occasional moments of satisfaction, mostly it's draining. Enervating, not energizing."

"I wish I could take a hiatus from work, from my life as it is now. I want to find myself again. I feel like everybody wants a piece of me. I'm an attorney, a wife, a mother. But who am I really?"

Sandy's gaze drifted to the kitchen window, outside where Chelsea and Justin romped, chased by a loping Stanley. The children shrieked with laughter, Stanley woofed in agreement.

"Reid and I had a big fight last night," Sandy said.

John rubbed the bridge of his nose and suppressed a heavy sigh. Sandy was telling him more than he wanted to know. He liked Reid. He'd always seemed like a thoughtful, decent guy who loved Sandy very much. He worked a lot, that was true, but he doted on the kids. If his sister and brother-in-law were having marital problems, he'd prefer to not be caught in the middle.

"I still don't know what it was about," she said. "He snapped at me for some trivial thing, I snapped back, and the next thing you know we were yelling and screaming at each other."

"When was the last time you two had a vacation?" John suggested, hoping to divert the conversation.

"It's been a while," she admitted. "But there's no way we can both get away for long."

"So take a weekend trip. Mom will watch Justin and Chelsea. Or I will."

Sandy rolled her eyes. "God forbid! I really haven't thanked you properly for teaching Justin those train noises."

"Don't mention it—that's what uncles are for." John grinned.

"Thanks." She lightly punched him in the shoulder. "Listen, I'd better let you get on with your date."

John glanced at the kitchen clock. Karyn would be arriving any minute. Sandy collected her son and daughter and ushered them to the front door. As John opened the door for his sister, he found Karyn on the threshold, her hand reaching for the buzzer.

Thoughts of his sister and her problems fled. John found himself grinning stupidly. "Right on time!"

Karyn's hair curled loosely about her shoulders. She wore a flowered blouse of some pinkish color tucked into a pair of blue jeans that hugged her legs. On her feet, she wore a pair of low-heeled boots.

"I live close," she answered, her gaze shifting beyond John to Sandy and the two children.

John introduced Karyn to his sister, who eyed Karyn with unabashed interest.

"I'd like to say I've heard a lot about you, but despite my best efforts to pump him for information, he refused to divulge much information," Sandy said, as she shook hands with Karyn.

"Brothers are that way," Karyn said. "Stubborn just for the sake of being so."

"Is that the voice of experience?" Sandy asked.

Karyn nodded. "I have an older brother."

Sandy shot a teasing glance at John. "John's my little brother."

As expected, he took the bait. "We're twins," he explained to Karyn. "Sandy is only minutes older than I am. Being the pushy person that she is, she insisted on being born first."

"Are you Uncle John's girlfriend?" Justin cut in.

"Justin, it's rude to ask personal questions like that." On cue, Sandy parroted a mild rebuke, but from her rapt gaze, he could tell she wanted to know the answer more than Justin did.

Karyn glanced at John, then looked at Justin. "At this point in time, I think I'm your uncle's friend."

"You're a girl. If you're his friend, then you must be his girlfriend," Justin insisted.

"It seems simple, sport, but it's lot more complicated than that." John ruffled Justin's hair.

"We'd better run. I've tormented you enough for one day," Sandy said.

His sister and niece and nephew left and John shut the door with exaggerated relief.

Karyn smiled. "It kind of makes you feel like sixteen again when your family wants to check out your date. My dad was cool, but my brother used to interrogate my dates mercilessly. I'm surprised anyone ever wanted to do out with me more than once."

His gaze was warm. "I doubt that any of your boyfriends would be easily deterred."

John watched as Karyn's gaze took in the living room. The old brick fireplace with the oak mantle created a warm, inviting focal point, drawing the eye away from the rest of the room, which testified to his lack of taste. Function, not style, dictated his choice of furnishings—that, and the availability of cast-offs donated by his family. Fortunately, he'd taken the time to straighten up a bit, tossing out a week's worth of newspapers, removing the thick coat of dust and running the vacuum.

"It's a little rough, but I only moved in five years ago," he joked self-consciously.

"It looks like my brother's place," Karyn said.

"Your brother and your family are in California?"

"My brother lives on the East Coast. My mom is in California. My dad died several years ago."

"I'm sorry," John said.

"It was a shock. It took me a while to get over it, but it hit Mom the worst. I think she's finally adjusting, though."

"Have a seat, and I'll, uh, get the stuff," he said. In the kitchen, he took several deep breaths and checked to see that he had everything, giving his nerves time to stop jitterbugging.

"Tres romantique!" she said in an exaggerated French accent when he returned with the basket.

"Mais oui. Vamos, Fraulein," he answered, using every foreign phrase he knew.

Karyn led the way to her Miata.

"Do you have a spot in mind?" she asked when they were settled and she'd donned a pair of sunglasses.

"I thought we'd just drive out of the city and find a place that looked inviting," he answered.

"I know a place. I go there sometimes when I want to get away. It's peaceful. We might even see some deer."

"Sounds perfect." John stretched his legs. "This looks like a fun little car."

"I won it on a game show."

"You're kidding!" John stared at her.

She smiled. "Do you ever watch *Trivia Q?*"

"*Trivia Q?!*" He did a double-take. *Trivia Q* tested contestants' knowledge of the mundane and arcane. He forgot what the Q stood for. Quiz, maybe? Or was it quotient? What ever it was, it was hard. Contestants had to be quick on the buzzer as well as smart. There was no time to mull over an answer.

"I'm impressed," he said. "How long were you on?"

"Five days."

"You were a champion!"

"Yeah." She sounded a little sheepish, but a satisfied smile rested on her lips. "I won the car in the Trivia Bonus Round." Undefeated champions had the opportunity to answer one last question to obtain a final prize.

"I wish I had seen you. Did you tape it?"

Karyn laughed. "My mom did. She sent a copy to all the relatives. If she had her way, it would be in video rental stores across the United States."

"I'd love to see it," John said.

"I'd sooner show you my vacation slides."

"I'd like to see those, too." Karyn in a bikini. Now there was a thought.

"Right!" she laughed.

"Really," he insisted. "That show is tough. It always makes me feel like such a dummy. How can people know all that stuff?"

"I crammed for weeks." Karyn checked her rearview mirror and began to pass a pickup truck driven by a grizzled old man who could barely see over the dashboard.

"What do you study for something like that?"

"*Cliff's Notes*, almanacs, phrase books—that sort of thing. It's mostly recall, not understanding. You know, like word association. They ask a question and something comes to mind. Sometimes you don't even know if it's correct, you just know that it's associated with that subject. And bingo! It turns out to be the right answer."

"Bingo I can do. *Trivia Q* is another story. How far away is this place you're taking us to?"

"Not far. Another ten minutes. We get off up here." She pointed to the numbered exit half a mile ahead. She turned on the radio. Mellow rock music poured softly from the dash. "What kind of music do you like?"

"All kinds. For a relative newcomer, you seem to know your way around Seattle," John said.

"When I moved here, I'd go for long drives. At first, I just wanted to get to know the area; then after my fiancé and I broke up, to get away."

"That must have been rough to be in a strange place alone."

"Yeah. But my friend—the one who placed the ad—saw that I got out. She made me do things even when I didn't want to. And I had my work."

At the bottom of the freeway offramp, Karyn turned right. "Cel was great. I don't always appreciate her efforts, but I know she has my best interests at heart. I have some friends I've known longer, but Cel is my closest friend."

"That's important. There's no substitute for friends. I have a friend from college, Bob Harrison. We're about as opposite as two people can be, but I'd take a bullet for him. And my sister. We give each other a hard time every chance we get, but I consider her to be one of my best friends."

They rode for a few miles on a paved road, then on a gravel track flanked by conifers. She slowed as the road turned sharply to the right, then veered off onto a dirt pathway, barely wide enough for the car.

"You do know where you're going, right?" John felt compelled to ask. He had no idea where he was.

"Of course. It's right up here. Past that tree." She pointed to a pine bowing over the road.

They neared the pine and the road widened to a bulge. Karyn pulled off to the side and cut the engine. "Now we walk."

Once out of the Miata, she extracted a woolen plaid blanket from the trunk. John grabbed the picnic basket and followed Karyn across tall grass to a slight path that cut through the trees.

* * *

"Well?" Panting slightly from the exertion, Karyn stood, hands on her hips, waiting for his evaluation. The walk had turned into a hike over fallen trees, through scratchy brush, and around boulders.

But it had been worth it. John surveyed the small clearing where they stood. Tall grasses carpeted a secluded meadow, the reeds undulating in the teasing breeze.

"Beautiful," he said, looking at Karyn. Her face glowed with the warmth of the sun. She looked young, happy, and exceedingly beautiful. John wondered if he risked kissing her now.

"Isn't the stream perfect?" Her arm swept out to encompass a little creek that had escaped John's notice.

"Wonderful." He feigned interest, finding Karyn

more riveting than the stream. "Water. Rocks. Probably a tadpole or two."

"Let's sit on that rock." Karyn pointed to a huge flat boulder that sat in the middle of the stream, forcing the rushing water to fork around it.

"I'll spread the blanket," he offered and handed her the basket. Gingerly, he stepped across the wet, slippery algae-covered rocks to spread the blanket over the boulder. "Basket," he commanded, reaching back.

Karyn passed it to him and he placed it on the rock.

"Let me help you up," he said.

She picked her way across the stones, arms extended for balance. Then she was there, in front of him, her perfume, a subtle, flowery fragrance mingling with the scent of the pine trees.

For a moment, he could only stare, transfixed.

"Is something wrong?" she asked.

"No. No. I'm just . . ." He shook his head. "I don't know what I'm doing."

John leaped onto the boulder, then reached down for Karyn's hand. With a tug, he helped her aboard. Her hand was soft and fit nicely in his.

"Thank you." Her eyelids lowered and John released her. He thought he detected a slight smile on her lips, but it was quickly gone.

"Wine?" he asked.

"Please."

Grateful for something to do, something to distract him, he proceeded to open the wine. Under her scrutiny, his fingers fumbled with the corkscrew, and he succeeded in breaking the cork in half, pushing it into the bottle.

"I should have paid extra and gotten wine with a

screw top," he said facetiously, eyeing bits of cork bobbing in the wine.

"That's okay, I like a little cork with my wine." Karyn smiled.

"I usually prefer to get my daily requirement of fiber in my breakfast cereal, but cork will do." John raised his glass. "A toast," he intoned. "To the start of something great."

Their plastic glasses clicked together and Karyn took a sip of her wine. "Good," she commented. "A delicate blend with a hint of oak."

"You know about wines?" John asked.

"I was reading the bottle," she admitted. "I wouldn't have done well on *Trivia Q* if the subject had been enology."

"Enology?" John cocked his head.

"The study of wines," she answered. "What else did you bring?"

"Bring?" He parroted dumbly.

"Food?"

"Oh! Yeah. Food."

"What a spread," she said, when he had laid out the food on the blanket. She opened a carton. "Marinated mushrooms! I love marinated mushrooms. There's this little place called Antonio's Deli that has wonderful—" She broke off at John's nod. "You got these at Antonio's?"

"I go there all the time." He often stopped on his way home, picked something up and ate in front of the TV.

"They have a pastrami sandwich that's to die for," she exclaimed.

"With extra peppers?"

She nodded vigorously.

"I'm surprised I never ran into you there," he mused.

"Maybe you did, but didn't notice me," she suggested.

"No." He was emphatic. "I would have noticed you."

He gazed at her for a long moment. His heart rate accelerated and his breathing quickened. He could feel the heat of the sun beating down on his back and neck, but the warmth he felt didn't come from the sun. Finally, she broke eye contact gaze and looked away.

"Chicken?" he asked.

"What?" Her head jerked around.

"Would you like some chicken?" He held out the foil-wrapped package.

"Thank you," she said and with a careful movement took the package from his hands.

She placed a piece of chicken on his plate and added a drumstick to hers. When all the food had been dished out, they began to eat.

"I never tire of coming here." Karyn stared at the trees and sipped her wine. "Places like this help you put things into perspective. This place does that for me. Do you have somewhere you can go just to reflect, to think, to be utterly and wholly yourself?"

John thought of the Other Side. "Yes," he answered. And because he didn't want to have to describe his private place, he thought it prudent to move on. "This spot is really out of the way. How did you find it?"

Karyn's lips curved into a sheepish smile. "I got lost. I was out driving around, made a wrong turn, and ended up on the road back there."

She paused, mulling something over in her mind.

"One reason I like to come here is that I see this place as a kind of metaphor for my life."

"How so?"

"I don't think of myself as one of those self-absorbed, ultrasensitive individuals who's continually searching for meaning. Life is what it is. Get over it and move on. But, that said, I found myself when I felt the most lost. And I found this place when I was literally lost."

"When everything familiar disappears, you can't rely on entrenched habits, and you become open to new possibilities, and new opportunities," John said.

"Exactly!" Her eyes shone.

In John's mind, this shared understanding forged a link between them, an invisible bond drawing them closer. More than ever, he regretted lying to her about his occupation. If anyone could understand what he did, Karyn would.

"Thank you," he said, and giving in to the impulse urging him since he'd met her, leaned over and kissed her. Her hand came up to cup the side of his face, one finger tracing his jaw.

"For what?" she asked, when they reluctantly ended the kiss.

For being you, sounded corny. "For being here," he said.

John scooted across the rock, moving closer. He wrapped his arm around her shoulders and hugged her tight against his chest. She fit perfectly, and he knew he'd been waiting for this since he'd seen her on the street.

They broke apart.

John could feel the corners of his mouth turn up and he knew he was grinning like a fool.

She smiled.

He felt happy. Stupidly, ridiculously happy.

He wasn't aware that they'd finished lunch, but they must have, because everything had been stowed in the basket. "How about a walk?" John stole another kiss.

"Through the stream?"

He chuckled. "Through the stream." He removed his shoes and rolled his pants legs up to the knees; she did likewise. John eased off the rock into the stream, fed by the mountain run-off of melted snow. The icy current chilled his feet, lapping at his calves.

Karyn slid off the rock into his arms and shrieked as her bare feet landed in the water. "It's cold!"

John couldn't resist another quick kiss before reaching up to snag the wine bottle, which he wedged between two stones in the creek.

"Natural refrigeration. Let's walk. Once you can no longer feel your feet, the cold is no problem." He entwined his fingers with hers.

With their hands firmly clasped, they waded through the stream, splashing like two kids, finding a puddle on a rainy day. Beneath his feet, the sandy bed felt gritty, but the stones were pleasingly smooth from polishing by the rushing water. Schools of tadpoles darted among the larger rocks. Through the clear, bracing water he could see Karyn's feet. She'd painted her toenails a bright pink.

The combined impact of her presence, the sun's warmth radiating on his head and shoulders, and the mellowing effects of the wine made him feel giddy and lightheaded, as if he'd overdosed on too much cold medicine. He wracked his brain for a witty comment, but all he could come up with was, "My feet are numb."

"Mine, too," she said.

They tiptoed across rocks, bent to examine a small school of guppies wriggling through the current, and skipped stones across the stream. John knew the day would be etched in his memory like an engraving on metal. Permanent.

With Karyn's hand in his, John couldn't help think of the bigger picture. She seemed to fit him so well. So many things had had to fall into place for them to meet.

"Isn't it funny that we live only blocks from each other, we met on the street while walking our dogs, and then I answered an ad your friend placed for you?" John asked.

"Quite a coincidence," she agreed.

"What if it's not?" he shrugged. "What if it's more than serendipity. What if it's fate?"

"I thought you didn't believe in fate?"

"I believe in fate. I just think we choose our own."

She shook her head. "If it's fate, you didn't choose it; it chose you. I prefer to think I have more control over my destiny."

Chapter
Eight

On the way home, they stopped at a roadside carnival, lured like moths to a flame by the bright lights of the Ferris wheel spotted from the highway. The tinny music floated toward them. John could almost smell the popcorn.

By the time they got to the ticket gate, he could. The carnival lit up the night like the Las Vegas Strip, a blinding array of swirling, blinking lights. His ears filled with the happy screams of fearless children and cowardly adults braving the whirling rides; the loud shouts of the carnival barkers trying to entice the carnival-goers to try their hand, three-for-a-dollar; and the gay music that seemed to go with the spinning kaleidoscope of lights. It evoked happy memories of his childhood, and John found himself eager to rush inside the gates as he paid for their tickets.

They rode the huge carousel, Karyn choosing a bright orange tiger, its body ablaze with color, its mouth open in a roar. John selected a traditional, but fiery stallion on the outside. As the ride neared its end, John lunged for the brass ring and victoriously rang the bell.

They savored foot-long New York hot dogs while standing in line for another ride and shared a cotton candy as they went round and round on the Ferris wheel. At the top, they had a view of the entire carnival and the city lights beyond. It was there that Karyn spotted the Hammer.

"I have to go on the Hammer. I love the Hammer!" She squirmed like a kid.

John had braved the tentacled Octopus, but that was before the hot dog, popcorn, lemonade, and cotton candy. He blanched at the thought of being tossed to and fro, up and down, back and forth.

"Uh . . ." he fumbled.

"It'll be fun," she urged, her eyes alight.

"I think that's one you better do without me."

"You don't mind?"

"Trust me." He smiled, relieved that she didn't demand that he go with her.

The Ferris wheel ride ended and she wove through the crowds to the Hammer. "Two?" asked the carnie when they reached the front of the line.

"One," John said as Karyn handed over her ticket. The carnie grinned, revealing a mouthful of yellowed stubs.

Karyn rushed to the cage, followed by two children pulling their rather harried-looking father. They and a woman of large proportions piled in with her.

The ride began with a slow rocking but picked up speed, swinging its passengers back and forth, the momentum hurling them 180 degrees straight up before gravity pulled them down to earth. Laughter turned to screams of delight the first time the Hammer descended. As the cage hurled past him, John could see Karyn's face wreathed in a smile as she joined the two kids in shouting "faster, faster." The father bore a gray and strained expression, and the rotund woman looked quite peaked.

John knew he had made the right decision.

The ride stopped and Karyn ran toward him, her face beaming. "That was so cool! You ought to try it."

"I don't think so." John eyed the other female passenger, helped from the cage by two carnies.

Karyn was still bubbling about the ride when John spotted the fortune-teller.

The sign promised that Madame Ilona could tell your future and fortune by tarot cards, palm reading or tea leaves. Mounted outside the gaudy colored tent was a poster of Madame Ilona peering intently into a crystal ball, either divining the future or suffering the deleterious effects of a migraine.

The odds of a carnival fortune-teller being to forecast anything but banal generalities equaled the odds of winning the lottery, thought John. But it could be fun.

"Want to have your fortune told?" he asked Karyn, only half-joking.

The laugh he'd expected from her didn't come. Instead, her mouth tightened. "I'll pass."

"What's wrong?" He eyed her pinched expression.

"People like that ought to be arrested."

"People like what?" He glanced around. "The fortune-teller? Why?" From the churning he suddenly felt in his stomach, he might as well have braved the Hammer.

"People shouldn't be allowed to prey on other people's vulnerabilities," she stated.

"She's just a carnival fortune-teller," he said. "No one expects Madame Ilona to be real."

"Maybe not her," Karyn conceded. "But people like her. People who call themselves psychics or mediums."

"You don't believe that there are people who do have legitimate psychic ability? Some people say that everyone has psychic ability, it's just latent."

"Those are the same people who are trying to sell you a reading for fifty bucks. The only ability so-called psychics have is the ability to take advantage of people. They've developed a skill at reading people. They notice when someone's pupil dilates, or their hand jerks in response to a question. That's all it is."

Derision in her expression, Karyn's focused on a man futilely throwing softballs at a pyramid of Coke bottles. The softball grazed the bottles, but they remained standing. He passed the carnie another dollar. "It's like that game. It's all a setup."

A sourness more acidic that the lemonade he'd drunk seemed to coat his mouth. "You sound so sure of this. Have you had a personal experience with a psychic?"

"Not me. My mother."

John exhaled in a loud whoosh, but Karyn didn't seem to notice. Her gaze clouded over and she starred straight ahead. When she spoke, her voice was wooden, flat.

"After Dad died, Mom went to pieces. She couldn't let go, wouldn't change a thing in the house, right down to the toothpaste cap he'd left on the sink the morning before he passed away."

"Then she found this spiritual advisor. It seemed harmless at first. The "psychic" told her Dad was all right and that made Mom feel good. We didn't know about the money Mom was spending. The bank was ready to foreclose on the house before my brother and I found out.

"She lost thousands of dollars. Her retirement would have been comfortable; now she's lucky to get by. If it wasn't for the money my brother and I send her each month, she wouldn't be able to."

John's hopes disintegrated like the cotton candy that had melted in his mouth, only the aftertaste was bitter.

"I'm sorry," he said, apologizing for many things Karyn wasn't even aware of, yet.

"No, I'm sorry," Karyn regained her composure, oblivious to John's turmoil. "I shouldn't have gone off like that."

Her gaze traveled over his shoulder and then her face brightened. "Hey, let's have our picture taken!" She steered him toward a photo booth, where for $10 they could have their photograph taken behind a cardboard cutout of costumed characters, real and fictional.

"Sounds great," John said with feigned interest. Karyn selected gangster and moll costumes. For an extra $5, they received an additional photo, one for each of them in a gaudily ornate frame.

They stayed late to watch the fireworks. There was something symbolic about rockets exploding into puffs of smoke—rather like his hopes, John thought.

On the way home, Karyn asked if he'd like to drive. He responded with forced alacrity, his heart not in it, occupied instead with Karyn's revelation. He recalled their conversation about fate, and the path he'd chosen by lying to her.

Outside his house, John turned off the ignition.

"I hope I didn't spoil things by running off at the mouth like that. It's just something I feel strongly about," she apologized.

"It's something I needed to know." He just wished she'd told him sooner.

Chapter Nine

Enroute to the Steak Out to meet Bob Harrison, his accountant and old college buddy, John stopped at a florist and ordered flowers for Karyn. "Thanks for a wonderful time. See you Saturday," he scribbled on the card.

He'd decided to ignore his common sense, which told him that a relationship with Karyn was doomed, and proceed full-steam ahead while he waited for the right time to tell her the truth. He liked her too much to give up now.

Bob was waiting when John arrived. "Hey, man, how the hell are you?" Bob bellowed, thumping John on the back.

"Great, just great," John answered, tapping Bob on the arm none too gently. "You've gotten uglier, though."

"Speak for yourself," Bob laughed.

The layout of the Steak Out formed a horseshoe, with tables and booths on both sides of the U. Western paraphernalia—branding irons, bridles, wagon wheels, stagecoach boxes—decorated the walls. En route to their table, Bob dropped his business card in a drawing for a saddle.

"You don't have a horse," John pointed out.

"So what? It's free," Bob said.

A waitress wearing cowboy boots, tight jeans and a Western shirt came to take their order. "So, what have you been doing with yourself?" Bob asked when she'd left.

John thought of Karyn. "The usual. Work."

"Did you catch the game on Sunday?" Bob lived for sports.

Karyn came to mind again. "No, I was busy."

Bob shook his head and quickly recapped the highlights. "Ten seconds left in the game, only ten yards to go, and the asshole drops the ball. Where do they find these morons? The guy earns six million dollars a year, and he can't hold onto a goddamn football."

"Sorry I missed it," John said.

Bob shook his head in disgust. "What could be so important that you'd miss the game?"

"I had a date."

Bob nodded in approval. "Getting laid is a good excuse."

"A first date."

"What does that have to do with anything?"

"You more than anyone else should know the answer to that," John jibed.

"Women are crazy about me." As Bob ran a hand over his balding head, the buttons strained to keep his shirt closed over his protruding beer gut.

"Listen to him!" John scoffed.

"If I wasn't married, the women would be all over me."

"You wish," John shot back. "How is Ellen?"

Bob had been married for ten years and had two sons. For all his talk, he was as devoted a family man as John had ever known. His wife, Ellen, shared his interest in sports. Even more, her interest extended beyond the armchair to the playing field.

"Great. She has a softball game this Saturday. The boys and I will be there to cheer her on."

The waitress brought their orders, a lean roast beef

sandwich for John and a half-pound bacon cheeseburger with fries and a beer for Bob.

"Going light, I see," John said.

"Who are you, my wife?"

"You know what that does to your arteries," John persisted.

Back when they were college sophomores, Bob's father, Frank, died of a heart attack at forty-seven. His father's death sent Bob into on a drinking binge that nearly resulted in him flunking out of college.

Desperate to help his friend, John risked exposure to contact Frank on the Other Side, mediating conversations between the two of them. Skeptical—even angry at first, believing that John was making fun of him—Bob gradually came to believe in his friend's ability. The experience halted the spiraling descent of his life.

It had had an equally profound impact on John. Through the mediation between Bob and Frank, John recognized and answered his calling. It was, in fact, what had started him traveling to the Other Side to help other people.

With the exception of John's family, Bob remained the only person with whom John truly shared the knowledge of his travels and was the only one who believed him.

Bob took a swig of his beer. "So how's the spook biz?"

"It's complicating things," John admitted. "A woman came to me wanting me to contact her dead husband. Turns out there is no husband. She's a cop with the Seattle P.D."

"No shit?"

"I think they think I'm after little old ladies' pension checks or something."

"They can make it rough for you."

"I'm not worried. I haven't done anything illegal."

"Tell me about this woman you're seeing. Is she a looker?"

A picture of Karyn in white shorts and a red sweatshirt, the way she had looked when he'd first laid eyes on her, flashed through his mind. "Yeah."

"Big tits?"

"Blond," John answered.

Bob laughed. "That means yes. Is she a client?"

"I never date clients, you know that. I met her jogging. Stanley ran her cat up a tree." John thought it prudent to omit he'd answered a personal ad.

"And you asked her out. And being that you're a complete stranger and quite possibly a homicidal maniac, she said yes immediately. What's her name?"

"Karyn with a Y."

"Karen with a Y. Interesting last name—WithaY. What nationality is that?" Bob smirked.

"Asshole," John countered. "Her last name is Walker."

"Does she know what you do?"

John looked down at his plate. "That's a problem."

Bob stopped eating. "Like a dumb shit, you didn't tell her, right?"

"It's worse than that." John sighed. "Her mother was scammed by a psychic. We went to a carnival and I jokingly suggested she get her fortune read. She went ballistic. I'm not a psychic, but I don't think Karyn will see the distinction."

"So does she think you're chronically unemployed? What does she think you do?"

"I told her I was a communications consultant."

Bob choked on a French fry. "How long do you think you can go on seeing her before she finds out?"

"I'm going to tell her before that happens."

"And because you're so charming and handsome, she'll forgive you for being what she considers to be the scum of the earth, and for lying to her about it."

"Something like that."

John looked away from Bob's disgusted stare, and glanced around the restaurant. The typical business-suited lunch crowd was in attendance, the men with meals similar to Bob's, the women with salads. John's gaze skimmed over a couple in a corner booth, then shot back.

The woman leaned toward her male companion, the jacket of her navy blue designer suit unbuttoned to reveal a hint of lace-covered cleavage. Something the man said struck her as funny, because she laughed, low and throaty, and caressed the back of his hand with one daggered fingernail.

Bob followed John's stare. "Looks like he's getting some."

"That's my brother-in-law," John said quietly.

"Your sister looks different from what I remember." Bob stuffed the last bite of cheeseburger into his mouth. "That's not my sister."

"Ah . . . a luncheon rendezvous . . ." Bob started to joke, then caught John's scowl. "It's probably nothing. A business lunch."

"Does that look like the kind of business lunches you have?"

"I've never been that lucky."

John tossed his napkin on the table and started to push back his chair.

"What are you doing?" Bob's head shot up.

"I'm going to say hello."

Bob grabbed John's arm as he started to rise. "Don't make me tackle you. Sit down, finish your lunch, and mind your own business. What do you think you're going to do anyway? Punch him out right here?"

"That's not a bad idea."

"It's a terrible idea."

No wonder Reid was never home. He wasn't the first guy to cheat on his wife, but it seemed worse when the wife in question was your sister. What was he going to tell Sandy? She was going to be devastated.

"And for God's sake, don't say anything to your sister." Bob must have read his mind.

"I can't pretend I don't know anything." John recalled his sister's distress. "She knows something's not right. She needs to know what's really going on."

"Not from you. The odds are she already knows but isn't ready to face it. Butt out."

Reluctantly, John settled back against the booth. "Sandy was just telling me the other day she wished she had more romance in her marriage."

"Be cool, John," Bob hissed.

"I'm not doing anything, okay?" John snapped.

"I mean now. Brother-in-law at two o'clock."

"John!" Reid called, as he approached the table, the woman at his side. "I couldn't believe it, when I looked over here and saw you. What brings you to this part of the town?" His tone was even, his words casual, but John detected a paleness underneath Reid's tan and a small tic flickered under Reid's left eye.

"Lunch," John answered smoothly, though his gaze shot accusing darts at Reid. Though his sister had the relationship with Reid, John felt as if he were the one who'd been betrayed. He'd liked Reid, had thought he and Sandy were well suited for each other.

A slight flush darkened Reid's features as he caught the censure. His companion reacted coolly, her chin rising to the challenge. She regarded John steadily for a moment, then looked away as if she'd found him lacking.

John sized her up as well.

Piranha.

From the tip of her alligator pumps to the straps of her snake skin shoulder purse, everything about her cried "man-eater."

"This is my *associate*, Caitlin Mitchell," Reid introduced her, hovering for a moment on the word associate. "Caitlin, this is my brother-in-law, Reid, and—"

"Bob," his friend cut in. "Bob Harrison at your service." He shook hands with Reid and Caitlin and, ignoring the glare John directed at him, reached into his shirt pocket and extracted a couple of business cards.

"Well, we'd better get back to work. I'll talk to Sandy and we'll have to have you over for dinner. Soon."

"That would be . . . interesting," John said.

"Great. Nice meeting you, Bob." Reid said politely.

John watched as Reid and his associate-piranha-lover departed. "Shithead," he said, underneath his breath.

"Remember what I told you," Bob warned. "Keep your big mouth shut."

"I have to do something."

"If it makes you feel better, beam over to the Other Side and zap the guy with a lightening bolt."

* * *

Though his first instinct was to call Sandy immediately, John decided to take Bob's advice for the time being and do nothing. But the incident lingered in his mind and competed for his attention with thoughts of Karyn. She was, perhaps, the only thing that kept him sane as everything started to go awry, like springs popping out of an old sofa.

First fire department officials dropped in, a seemingly innocuous blip on the screen of an average day. John was in the middle of a session with a client, "in a trance," his head slumped to his chest, when he heard the bell up front jingle.

He wrapped up the session and went to see who'd entered his office. The uniformed fire inspector waited as he escorted the client to the door.

"We're here to do a fire inspection," the inspector informed him.

"I had an annual inspection two months ago," John protested.

"We've since had reports of fire violations."

"From who?"

"They don't tell us who. They just tell us to check it out."

"What kind of violation?" John asked.

"Overcrowding," said the inspector.

"You're joking," John exclaimed, glancing around the deserted room furnished with the barest of essentials.

The inspector wasn't.

He combed the three-room suite and then cited John for an expired fire extinguisher and said he'd be back to check.

Next, his Explorer was ticketed for being parked too far from the curb.

But the final blows were delivered by the U.S. Post Office in the afternoon mail. Two letters: one from the city informing him that his business license was being reviewed, the other from the Internal Revenue Service. His business deductions for the last three years were being audited.

Chapter
Ten

John crashed onto the sofa, his energy sapped by the past week that had been spent fixing problems that materialized out of nowhere. His entire life had turned into an accident waiting to happen.

He'd contacted the city about his business license and had been informed the review was part of a random audit to determine if local businesses were complying with zoning and other ordinances. But when he asked how many businesses were being audited, the official didn't have that information. And several careful queries among the other business owners on his street revealed that none of them were being audited.

The fire inspection, the business license review, the tax audit. John realized he was being targeted, like a six-point bull elk during hunting season.

"When it rains, it pours," John said aloud and picked up the phone. He and Karyn had weekend plans, but he needed to hear a friendly voice before then.

Her phone rang four times and then picked up. His spirits dropped as he realized he'd gotten her machine. *"Hi! You've reached 555-6474. I am unable to come to phone right now, but if you leave your name—"*

"Hello?!" Karyn's voice broke in on the recording—"a *message, and phone number at the tone—*" The machine droned on.

"Hi! It's me." He paused. "John."

"I'll return your call as soon as I can—"

"John!" she said, and he could tell she was pleased to hear from him. "Darn it. I can't seem to turn this thing off."

"Have a nice—" There was a click and then silence.

"That's better," she said. "I just walked in—my key was still in the door when I heard the phone."

"If you're busy . . ."

"No. It's okay."

"Actually, I figured it was a long shot. I didn't think you'd be home yet."

"Do you always call people when you think they won't be home?" Humor warmed her words.

"I hoped listening to your voice on the answering machine would tide me over until I could see you again," he answered. "Are you smiling?" he asked.

"What?"

"Are you smiling? I have this image of you smiling."

"Maybe." Her answer was noncommittal, her tone amused. "Why?"

"Because I am," he confessed.

"Oh."

"I'll bet you're smiling now."

"Maybe." Suppressed laughter lightened her voice. "What are you, psychic?"

"Let's just say I have special powers."

"Like Superman?"

"Well, no one's ever called me _that_ before," John chuckled.

"I've been thinking about you."

"Good thoughts, I hope," he said.

"The best."

"Been thinking about what you want to this

Saturday?" he asked. "There's a place downtown called
The Siren that has a really cool mud-wrestling show."
"Sounds like a winner."
"Maybe after that, we could catch the late night
roller derby." He could feel himself grinning.
"Wonderful."
"Or, if you would prefer, I could rent the com-
plete video library of Seahawks half-time shows. We could
watch those, drink generic beer and belch."
"Given the options, it's so difficult to choose,"
Karyn laughed.
He paused. "I called you yesterday. I got
your machine."
"You didn't leave a message."
"I wanted to talk to you," he admitted. "Not your
machine. Saturday is a long way off." He couldn't count
the number of times he'd thought about Karyn in the past
week. Whatever he did, wherever he went, thoughts of
her intruded. Warm thoughts, affectionate thoughts, sexy
thoughts. Especially sexy thoughts.
"So don't wait until Saturday. Come over tonight."
"Well, I did kind of plan on color-coordinating
my sock drawer, but I guess I could do that another night.
When should I come over?"
"Anytime."
"I can be there in thirty minutes."
"Perfect. I'll throw something together
for dinner."
"Don't go to any trouble. We can grab a bite some-
where," he said.
John hung up, took the stairs two at a time, and
shrugged off his clothes into a heap on the bedroom floor.
He showered quickly, then shaved slowly, taking
care not to nick himself. It didn't make a good

impression to show up at a woman's house with toilet paper stuck to your face. He slapped on some after-shave, then pulled on a pair of gray cotton twill pants and a dark green shirt.

Standing on Karyn's front door, he took a deep breath before ringing the doorbell, suddenly attacked by a case of nerves. He steeled his courage and pushed the button. He heard the bell chime and moments later the door opened.

Karyn's blond hair fell softly around her face. Her lips curved into a smiled, lighting up her green eyes. She wore a pair of cobalt-blue linen slacks and a lacy white blouse with wide sleeves.

John was struck both by her attractiveness and the folly of his actions. What would happen when she found out what he did? One of these days he was going to have to tell her the truth.

But not tonight.

He stepped inside.

"Sorry I'm late," he said. "I stopped off at the store and there was a line. Here—" He handed her a bouquet of flowers and a bottle of wine.

"Thank you. You didn't have to do that."

The hairball called Missy sniffed at his shoes, while Suki the cat ignored him, passing by with only the slightest twitch of her tail to indicate she'd even registered his presence.

"Let me put the flowers in water. Would you like a glass of wine?" Karyn headed for the kitchen.

"Sure. What kind do you have?"

Karyn looked at the bottle in her hand. "White zinfandel."

"Perfect! Let me help you." He followed.

As Karyn arranged the flowers in a vase, John opened the wine.

John approached her, handing her the glass. "Here you go. It's a little low on fiber today," he joked, calling attention to the lack of cork pieces. "I don't think I said hello properly." Holding his glass steady, he leaned in and kissed her. "I missed you." The words tumbled out before he could stop them.

"I missed you, too." Karyn smiled over the rim of her glass. "Let's go into the other room."

They set their drinks on the low cocktail table and, by tacit agreement, sat closely together on the sofa.

"How has your week been?" he asked.

"Fine. Yours?"

"A little hectic," he answered.

"What kind of clients do you work with?" She settled back against the cushions of the sofa.

"Mostly old ones," he said, without thinking.

"Old ones?" She stared at him.

"I, uh, meant old, established businesses. But small ones," he fabricated. "Mom-and-pop businesses who need assistance adjusting to the new way of doing things. Diversity issues, ADA—American Disabilities Act—those types of changes."

What was wrong with him? He knew he had to 'fess up to the truth, and here he was telling more lies. If only she hadn't caught him by surprise. If only he hadn't told her he was a communications consultant!

"How's your job going?" he asked, not out of politeness or interest, but to divert the conversation from his work.

"Today was the first day I was able to leave work on time."

He'd spent the morning with Bob going over tax records and the afternoon at the city business licensing department and in between managed to squeeze in a couple of sessions with clients. "I know how that goes," he said. "Are you hungry? I could fix something . . ."

John shook his head. "Later. We'll order out."

He held her hand, caressing her palm with his thumb. She wore the same perfume she'd worn the day of the picnic, a subtle scent that invited him to lean closer. He shifted his position, and she met him half way.

"You smell nice," she said between kisses.

"Me too," he said. "I mean, you too."

"I know what you mean." Karyn laughed, and trailed a line of kisses along his jaw and down his throat.

He closed his eyes, enjoying the sensation. "You know where this is going to lead, don't you?"

"I hope so." She smiled. "I'd hate to think I called you over here for nothing."

Suddenly, his week improved.

* * *

Karyn's hands slowly circled his back as they lay twined together on the bed, one of her legs wedged between his. John's hand wound in her hair, playing with the silky strands.

At some point, Suki had jumped on bed and lay at their feet purring, a sound of contentment that seemed to echo throughout him. He didn't know what the cat had to purr about, but he had plenty.

In the short time that they'd known each other, Karyn had become very important to him. She filled a need and he felt connected to her.

He hugged her tight. "Thank you."

She lifted her head from his chest and peered at him. "For what?"

"For being here." He kissed her.

"It's not such a hardship." Her eyes crinkled, and she snuggled back down.

John held his breath, then took the dive. "What if it was? A hardship, I mean? What if I were involved in something you found unconscionable?"

"Is this a confession?" Her head lifted again.

He was trying to make it one, but the directness of her gaze made him feel like an unworthy bacteria specimen under a microscope. He shrugged. "We've had a lot of good times together."

John paused, choosing his words carefully. "I think we share some common interests, and I feel I'm getting to know you more. I like what I see. But I'm sure there are certain things that I don't know about you and that you don't know about me."

Karyn sat up. "You're not trying to tell me you're married?"

"No."

"Girlfriend?"

"No."

"Boyfriend?"

"No." John smiled, despite the seriousness of the situation.

She lay back down, but propped herself up on one elbow. "Does it affect the present?"

A straight yes would have cut to the chase, but John wavered. "That depends on you," he said. He stretched his legs and dislodged the cat who gave him the evil eye before leaping from the bed.

"John, what are you trying to say? What's going on here?"

"Hypothetically, what if you found out I was a junk bond trader or a psychic? What would you do?"

"If you were a junk bond trader, I'd help you get help. If you were psychic, well, I guess you'd be beyond help," her tone was light, but the meaning was clear.

"Is being a psychic such a terrible thing?" he asked. "I know your mother had a bad experience, but can you really judge all people based on that one experience? I mean there are good teachers and bad. Honest mechanics and dishonest mechanics. Psychics are the same."

"I think this is one area where we're going to have to agree to disagree," Karyn said. "I try to be an open, accepting person, but on this issue I'm not. I guess that's something about me and my past, that you ought to know."

John met her eyes. "Don't you believe in an afterlife?"

"A lot of people do," Karyn answered.

"But do *you*?" he pressed.

For a long moment she was silent. He waited.

"I don't know," she said, finally. "Do you?"

"Absolutely," he said, conviction ringing in his tone.

"What makes you so sure?"

Because I've been there. "Some things you just know. From my limited time on this earth, I know that there is a force, a life-force out there that is bigger, grander and more infinite than anything we could possibly imagine."

The image of the light filled his mind. He thought of his grandmother and Mr. Boswell and all the other souls on the Other Side that existed in the light, that *were* the light. His thoughts brought him peace and, contrarily anxiety also, because it wasn't something that he could share with Karyn.

"God," she summarized his description.

"You'd call it God."

"What would you call it?"

John shook his head. "I don't have a name for it. I just know that it exists."

"I wish I had your faith," she said. "But I think we've gotten off track. What secret lurks in your past that you want to tell me about?"

John shook his head, chose his words carefully. "I've tried to live my life as a good person. Do the right thing. Follow the rules." His lie to Karyn needled him. "Most of the time. I've slipped occasionally," he said.

"Who hasn't?"

There was no way he was going to be able to broach the subject in a roundabout way. He needed to just tell her. Just spit it out. On the count of three.

One.

Two.

"What about that dinner you enticed me over here with?" John asked.

They ordered Chinese food from a little neighborhood take-out joint and ate in bed, passing the cartons back and forth between them. When they finished, they broke open their fortune cookies.

"I feel cheated," Karyn said, looking at her fortune. "All I got was a word!"

John peered over her shoulder. *Trust,* her cookie said.

"A one word fortune isn't much to go on," Karyn complained. "What does your say?"

"*Little lies grow,*" John read reluctantly.

Chapter
Eleven

Wedged between two office towers in the financial district of Seattle, The Tea House stood as an anomaly among the glass and steel edifices. A tiny building with a canopied exterior, it was a popular luncheon spot for the businesswoman crowd. The interior was decorated in a cluttered Victorian style that made the restaurant seem even smaller than it was but somehow added to its cozy charm.

Karyn sat by the window where she could watch pedestrians while waiting for Celine whom she was meeting for a long overdue lunch. A few minutes later, Celine blazed in and made her way to the table.

"Sorry I'm late. I got tied up at the station," she explained, sliding into the empty chair. "Hope you haven't been waiting long."

Karyn shook her head. "Just got here. I ordered you a mineral water with lime." She indicated a glass on the table.

"Thanks. It's been a long time since I've seen you. Where have you been hiding yourself?"

"I've been kind of busy."

"You look great," Celine said.

"Thank you. So do you, but you always do."

Celine picked up the menu and perused it silently for a moment. "Do you know what you're going to get?"

"Raspberry chicken. You won't find it on the menu. It's the special."

Celine swiveled to look at the chalkboard listing the daily specials. "That sounds good. I'll have that, too."

After the waitress took their order, Celine turned to Karyn. "Now, I'm serious. This is your old friend Celine. I haven't seen you in six weeks and was beginning to think I was going to have to have lunch with your answering machine. Who's the guy?"

Karyn laughed. "Celine, you can be a real pain in the ass, but you're good."

"Don't try to distract me with compliments. Spill it."

"What do you want to know?"

"For starters, how did you meet and how long have you been seeing each other?"

"About a month and half, and I first met him while walking Missy." Karyn didn't feel the least bit guilty about withholding information about the personal ads.

"_First_ met him? What does that mean?"

Inwardly, Karyn cringed and rushed to the repair the damage. "I mean I met him walking the dog, and then we met at a coffee shop."

"Ah." Celine leveled an assessing gaze on Karyn. "What does he do for a living?"

"He's a communications consultant."

"What's his name?"

"John M—" Karyn broke off, staring at the notebook Celine had dug out of her purse. "What are you doing?"

"I'm going to check him out for you. Run him through the computer, make sure he doesn't have a criminal record and isn't wanted for anything. His name is John—"

"You will not." Karyn stared at her.

"Karyn—"

"Celine. You were the one who put the ad in the personals. And now you want to want to run my boyfriend through the computer?"

"Just like I would have done with any guy you met through the personals. It doesn't hurt to screen these guys."

"John doesn't need to be screened. I trust him. He wouldn't do anything to hurt me."

"What's the name of the communications business your friend owns?"

"I'm not telling you. Leave him alone," Karyn said, relieved to see the waitress bringing their order. The entrée, a tender marinated chicken breast resting on a bed of greens, looked and tasted delicious.

"What's he look like?" The arrival of lunch offered only a brief and temporary relief. Celine would not be diverted for long.

"Tall. Blond. Funny. Humble. He's not real full of himself like a lot of men are." Karyn smiled.

"If you won't let me run him through the computer, maybe I could have this psychic I know check him out," Celine laughed.

Karyn stared. "You're seeing a psychic?"

"The man in question is a suspect in a scam. We've had complaints about him. His *specialty* is contacting dead relatives. He has a regular clientele. He pretends to take their messages to Granny or Great Aunt Zelda or whomever and brings back a reply.

"The guy is real slick. Unfortunately, we couldn't get any hard evidence that he's doing anything illegal. We spoke to several of his regular customers. Some refused to talk to us, others sang his praises."

"So what can you do?" Karyn asked.

"Let's say the system will take care of him. His

life will be pretty uncomfortable in the months to come and we'll be watching him."

Celine toyed with the ice in her glass. "How's your mother these days?"

"Okay. She's working at Wal-Mart now, as one of those greeters." Thinking about it made Karyn angry. If not for the psychic who'd preyed on her vulnerability, Karyn's mother wouldn't have to work at all.

"My brother and I try to send her money when we can. At least she didn't lose the house." Karyn's mouth tightened. "I hope you get this guy."

"We will. One way or another. Don't worry."

Chapter
Twelve

Though it had been a while since John had visited the Other Side for a chat, his grandmother greeted him warmly.

"Johnny!" She enveloped him in a mental hug. "You finally decided to come visit your old grandma. It's been a long time," she chided gently. "Tell me about the girl."

His grandmother already knew everything she needed to know; her purpose was to get John's perspective.

"She's great," he said. "She's funny, warm, smart, sexy, independent. She works at the hospital with bereaved families, counseling patients, arranging for services." He paused. "I haven't told her I come here. I don't think it will go over well when I do."

A couple of months had passed since they'd begun seeing each other, and any admission on his part would be more of a confession.

"Will the situation improve the longer you wait?"

He sighed. "I don't know how to tell her."

"You need to tell her right away. Don't delay."

John sensed an urgency. "Why?"

"Because it's the right thing to do."

He could envision the scenario. *Hello, Karyn. Don't you look lovely tonight. I've been meaning to tell you something. I may have misspoke about myself. Remember when I said I was in communications? We'll I'm really a messenger. A psychic messenger. I carry messages and chess moves between people and their dead relatives. Get out, you say?*

"How's Sandy?" His grandmother inquired casually, but John knew it wasn't an idle question.

"She's fine. For now. I think Reid is having an affair. I saw him, in what appeared to be a romantic interlude, with another woman."

"You think Sandy doesn't know."

John shook his head. "I don't think so. She knows something's not right. She told me months ago he was working late a lot and didn't spend much time at home."

"And you've not said anything to Sandy about your suspicions?"

This was another of those situations in which the right words seemed to duck and hide. "I'm not even sure he *is* having an affair. He could have been just having lunch with a coworker. I didn't see how my suspicions could help."

"The truth is in front of her," his grandmother said. "Always remember that fate is a path we choose to follow."

"Do you really choose your fate if you can't see the end of the path?"

"First of all," his grandmother said in that patient voice she used to use with him when he was child, "there is no end to fate. It's infinite. There is no final destination. Secondly, the road is marked by signs. It's up to you to follow them or change course."

A star of light appeared in his consciousness and John knew that they weren't speaking about Sandy at all. His grandmother's next words confirmed it.

"The answers to your difficulties exist, John. They're as plain as the exit signs on the highway."

"What you're saying is that Sandy and I are each on a path of our own making. And we need to decide if we want to go where we're headed."

"That's right," she nodded. "I understand you survived your IRS audit."

"Barely." He grimaced. "It was a tough sell. I showed them receipts for my deductions. But I don't need to tell you they had me sweating. I still might lose my business license. It's under review. I can't understand why all this is happening at once."

"Things that seem to fly out of left field have a cause and usually announce their existence long before they arrive," she said.

"Another of those road signs?"

"Yes."

"Well I certainly missed this one."

"Tell me more about Karyn. About her family," his grandmother said.

"She has one older brother. He's a newspaper reporter back east. I haven't met him. Her mother was a homemaker, her father an executive with an aerospace company. He died of a heart attack several years ago. On the advice of a so-called psychic, Karyn's mother got involved in a pyramid scheme and lost most of her retirement nest egg. Which is the basis of my problem."

"The basis of your problem is that you lied to her."

John winced. His grandmother never let him get away with anything.

"What about friends?" his grandmother asked. "Have you met each other's friends? Have you met her mother? Has she met Steven and Nydia?"

"No. Her mom lives in California. I'm afraid to have her meet Mom and Dad. You know how Dad is; he's likely to say anything. And if I brought a girl home, Mom would have wedding invitations in the mail by the next morning. Karyn and I have been so occupied with each other that we haven't involved our friends and family."

"Your friends and family are involved. You just don't know it yet. You've left a lot of loose ends that need to be tied up before you get entangled any further."

Thirteen Chapter

Karyn linked her arm through his as they strode up the walk to his parents' house. She didn't seem the least bit nervous to be meeting his parents. His nerves, however, felt like a twisted tangle of fishing tackle.

But his grandmother was right; it was time that Karyn met his family. Even if he could ignore his grandmother's urging, Karyn had begun to ask questions about them and was getting suspicious as to why they hadn't been introduced.

"You do have parents, right?" she had asked.

"Two."

"They live in Seattle?"

"Bothell," he corrected, naming a Seattle suburb.

"You're on speaking terms?"

He thought for a moment. "Good enough."

"They're not axe murderers?"

"Not that I know of."

"So why haven't I met them?"

So here they were. If all went well, they'd all get acquainted in a safe, superficial manner, have dinner, and then duty fulfilled, John and Karyn could be on their way, relationship intact.

He feared it was too much to hope for.

They reached the front step. Before he could knock, the door flew open and his mother's beaming face appeared.

"Come in." The welcome in Nydia's voice pulled

them into the house. "You must be Karyn." His mom threw her arms around Karyn in a hug. "It's so nice to finally meet you. We've heard so much about you."

John hadn't told her anything except Karyn's name, that he had been seeing her for a while, and he'd like to bring her by to meet them.

"Well, here they are!" John's father rose from his chair. "I'm Steve, John's dad." He held out his hand to Karyn.

"She knows that, Steve," Nydia said.

"It's very nice to meet you," Karyn said. "I've been looking forward to this."

"Us too. We don't get to meet many of John's girl-friends." Nydia looked pointedly at John, then smiled at Karyn.

"Do you ever watch *News Flash?*" Steve drew Karyn to the sitting area. John followed closely, not want-ing to leave Karyn's side.

"I'm not home much," she answered politely.

"Tape it. You have a VCR, don't you? Everybody has a VCR." Steve's eyes gleamed. "They had a really good show the other night about a psychic who worked for a city police department—Minneapolis, Milwaukee, Montgomery—one of those M places—who turned out to be a fraud."

"Would you like some nuts, dear?" Nydia held out a can.

"Uh, sure. Thank you." Karyn helped herself to a few.

"Soda? Wine? Beer?"

"No, thank you."

"I'll have a beer." His dad stretched out in the re-cliner and picked up the remote.

"It's in the refrigerator," Nydia told him. To Karyn

she said. "Are you sure you wouldn't like a glass of wine?"

"I'm sure. Thank you."

"She's fine, Mom," John said.

"I'll go finish dinner." His mother placed the can of mixed nuts on the coffee table.

"Is there anything I can do to help?" Karyn asked.

"Don't be silly." His mom dismissed the idea with a wave.

Karyn seated herself on the sofa; John started to follow suit, but stopped when his mother called from the kitchen.

"John? Could you give me a hand, please?"

He sighed. "I'll be right back." He placed a light hand on Karyn's shoulder and shot his father a pleading look.

"Is *News Flash* your favorite show?" John heard Karyn ask as he left the room.

"She seems very nice." His mom diced vegetables for the salad.

"She is," he acceded. "What would you like me to do?"

"Nothing."

"Then why did you call me?"

"I thought we could talk. Just the two of us." She sliced avocado.

"Mom, Karyn is out there," he pointed toward the living room, "alone with Dad. The TV is on, but there could be a commercial at any time."

"Now what's the point of bringing a girl home if you're not going to let us get to know her? How long have you two been seeing each other?" Not one to waste time, his mother launched into the interrogation.

He should have prepared a social resume. *Karyn Walker. Medical Social Worker. Objective: To meet boyfriend's parents. Qualifications: Alive. Unmarried. Likes children. Experience: Worked as a camp counselor. Did some baby-sitting as a teenager.*

"Three months."

"What does she do?"

"She's a camp—I mean, a medical social worker at Seattle Hospital." He strained to hear to the conversation coming from the other room. All he could detect was the television.

"Does she want children?"

"Mom!" Full attention. "Karyn and I haven't even discussed marriage, let alone children. We've only been going out three months. Not even."

"Your father and I only dated for six weeks before he proposed."

"Mom, please. Not tonight, okay?"

His mother regarded him steadily. "I just want to be a grandmother before I get too old to enjoy grandchildren."

"Mom, you are a grandmother. Remember Justin and Chelsea?" he shot over his shoulder as he pushed through the swinging door that separated the kitchen from the dining area.

"And then I told them, 'The ad said it was fifty-inch TV. This is only a forty-five-inch. I want a fifty-inch TV,'" Steve was saying as Karyn uh-huhed politely.

A slow slide of pink goo oozed over the television screen, introducing an antacid commercial. His father zapped it with the remote. A celebrity appeared holding a box of hemorrhoid suppositories. Zap. A group of black basketball players bounced across the screen while the television blared a raucous, grating rock tune. It was either an ad for athletic shoes or hamburgers. His dad's eyes narrowed and his hand with the remote lowered to his lap. He must have decided it was hamburgers.

"What happened?" Karyn asked.

"I made them give me the fifty-inch TV they had advertised," Steve boasted.

"Good for you!" Karyn said.

"Service isn't what it used to be," Steve continued, warming to one of his favorite topics. "It used to be the customer is always right. Now?" Steve grunted disgustedly. "They don't care. Nobody's interested in doing an honest day's work for an honest day's pay. Kids these days don't want to pay their dues."

The commercials ended and jangling bells introduced the return of *News Flash*. John took a seat next to Karyn and clasped her hand, giving it a squeeze. "Sorry I deserted you like that."

"No problem. I had a very nice conversation with your dad."

That Karyn was still speaking to him seemed to indicate that his father hadn't said anything he shouldn't, but there was no need to take chances. "Let's sit on the porch," he suggested. "Get a little fresh air."

Once outside, John steered Karyn to the swing. They sat touching, his arm around her shoulders. The swing creaked as they rocked.

"You don't get along with your father, do you?" Karyn's seemingly casual query struck a bull's-eye.

John squirmed. One thing he'd learned in the months he'd dated Karyn was that she could be extremely perceptive. "What makes you say that?"

"The vibes." She paused. "I sense an awkwardness between the two of you."

"We don't see eye to eye. He doesn't approve of me."

"And he, of course, has your full and unconditional approval."

"Yeah—" John started to agree, but was stopped by Karyn's expression of disbelief. "Well, no," he admitted.

"There you go. Acceptance goes both ways. I think he'd like a better relationship with you."

"You got all this by watching ten minutes of television with him?"

"Don't be sarcastic."

"Sorry. It's just that he doesn't act like he cares."

"Maybe he doesn't know how. Maybe you need to make the first move." Karyn paused. "John, you never know what's going to happen. My dad died, and a day doesn't go by that I don't think about him. There are things I wish I had said that I never did. Don't make the same mistake. I'm sure your father loves you, but doesn't know how to show it."

"You don't understand. There's a lot that . . . " he searched for the right words and came up lacking. "You don't understand."

"Because you don't tell me. There's a part of you that you hold back. I can feel it."

What could he say? It was true. "Karyn—" he studied their entwined hands. "You're right. There is a part of me I'm holding back."

Their eyes connected.

John knew he'd reached that destination he's selected when he'd chosen this particular path. The time to come clean had arrived.

"I'll explain everything, but I want to do it right. Trust me, okay?"

Eyes wide, she nodded solemnly.

* * *

"This is wonderful, Nydia." Karyn praised the chicken dish John's mom had prepared, a concoction of her own creation, a recipe so jealously guarded she'd refused to submit it to the annual fund-raising cookbook of the sorority she belonged to.

"Thank you, dear." Nydia beamed. "I'll give you the recipe."

"Nid is quite a cook." Steve rubbed his bulging stomach. "That's why I've put on a few extra pounds over the years."

"John tells me you're a medical social worker. How long have you been doing that?" his mother asked.

"About ten years. Since I finished my master's in social work. But I've only been at Seattle Hospital for about a year."

"How did you decide on medical social work?"

"I liked the medical field. I considered becoming a nurse for a while. I wanted a field where I could go to school, graduate and be trained for something. Medical social work seemed to be the ticket." Karyn took a sip of water.

"John has a degree in business," his mother said. "But you probably know that."

"Pass the potatoes, please," John said. He didn't like the direction the conversation was headed.

"Of course, what he does is a little unusual—" Nydia continued, oblivious to the panicked look on her son's face.

"Rolls!" John nearly shouted. "Mom, can I have the rolls, please?" The moment he'd feared began to unfold, like a knit sweater unraveling.

He'd struggled with what to tell his parents about

Karyn. To ask them not to say anything about his occupation would be tantamount to admitting he'd lied to his girlfriend. So, he hadn't told them anything. Hoping—desperately—that he could steer clear of any mention of his work.

"Steve, pass John the rolls," John's mom said, and continued without missing a beat. "As I was saying, it's a little unusual—"

"Butter, too!" John interrupted.

"John, you have a roll and butter on your plate, why do you want another one?"

"For later."

"What's unusual about being a communications consultant?" Karyn glanced from Nydia to John.

Heat flooded his face, and John examined his plate. The bomb had been dropped and he was sitting at ground zero. All that was left was detonation.

Five. Four.

"Who's a communications consultant?" Nydia's eyebrows drew together.

Three.

"John is." Karyn's head cocked one side in confusion. "Isn't that right?" Karyn glanced from Nydia to John. He met her gaze helplessly.

Two.

"The *business*." Steve spoke, stopping the timer the instant before the bomb exploded. "You know, Nydia. John's business." Steve focused on her face. "The one he started a few years ago. His *own* business."

His mother suddenly got the message. "Oh! Of course." She forced a laugh. "What am I thinking? You must think I'm going senile."

John could feel the blood pounding in his ears. He looked at his father, feeling grateful and ashamed all at once. His father regarded him steadily, sending the "look" he hadn't seen in years, the one that said they'd talk later.

"What do you do, Mr. Metcalf?" Karyn, for all her powers of perception, seemed unaware of the electricity that charged the room. Or maybe she was just too polite to say anything.

"Call me Steve. I'm a retired plumber."

"How long did you do that?"

"Almost thirty-five years. It was a good job, but I don't miss it. I'm enjoying retirement. Nid and I are hoping to travel a little. We want to buy one of those RVs and see the country."

"We want to see Mount Rushmore, Niagara Falls, Epcot Center, the Statue of Liberty," Nydia rattled off a list.

"I didn't know you guys wanted to travel." John had finally found his voice.

"There's a lot don't you don't know." Steve's look chided.

John caught Karyn's I-told-you-so glance.

"I haven't traveled that much," she said. "Just Hawaii and Mexico."

"I was stationed in Hawaii when I was in the Navy. Tried to get Nydia to come over for a rendezvous, but she wouldn't. We weren't married yet," Steve confided.

"I was only seventeen," Nydia said.

"And your dad had a shotgun." Steve laughed.

Nydia giggled like a teenager. "Pop would have made us get married the second our feet touched the mainland."

"I didn't know you wanted an RV," John blurted out. "How long have you been planning that?" He glanced from his father to his mother.

"Three, four years," Nydia answered. "Well, let me get this table cleared and I'll bring out dessert. We're having peach cobbler."

"I'll help you." Karyn jumped up and began to stack the dinner plates.

"Me too," John started to rise.

"Sit down. This will give me a chance to chat with Karyn," his mother said.

Silence filled the dining room after the women left. John knew how to deal with his father, the adversary. His father, the champion, created a whole new relationship.

"Thanks," John said. The word felt uncomfortable in his throat.

His dad nodded and regarded John steadily. "How come you haven't told her?"

John sighed. "I wanted to make a good impression and when she asked what I did for a living, the next thing I knew, I'd told her I was in communications."

"Son, you can't hide something like that."

"Maybe I didn't want her to think I'm a nutcase like you do."

A loud clink emanated from the direction of the kitchen, followed by the sound of running water and the hum of voices. Dishes were being washed and information exchanged. Dessert wasn't going to be served immediately.

"I'm sorry," his dad said quietly.

John's gawking stare brought a rueful smile to Steve's face. "You're my son and I love you and I want the best for you. I guess I didn't think that being a . . . psychic is good enough. What you do . . . it's all because of that time that we found you on the floor in your room and you said you had been to see Mom?"

John nodded.

"You scared us to death. We thought you were dead. For a month—hell, maybe two months—I'd check to see that you were okay two or three times a night. And then you kept trying to tell us how you could visit Grandma, a woman who'd been dead for a year."

Steve let out an audible sigh. "John, I'm a simple guy with average smarts. Maybe not even that. It was all more than I could handle. I knew there was something different about you, but I didn't want to admit it."

For a guy who usually communicated in grunts, it was quite a speech, and John didn't know how to react to this new side of his father.

Steve raked his hand through his hair. "I still don't understand what you do, how you do it, and frankly, I'm not even sure I believe it. But you're my son and I love you."

John felt a sting of tears well up in his eyes and he blinked them away. "I love you too, Dad." He looked around for a paper napkin to blow his nose, but they'd been picked up with the dirty dishes.

"You need to tell this woman of yours the truth. Starting off with lies between you is no way to build a solid relationship."

John exhaled. "Her mother was duped by someone claiming to be psychic."

"All the more reason to tell her. She likes you. A lot. I can tell. She'll come around. She may be mad as hell—and she has reason to be—but she'll come around. The longer you wait the harder it will be, and the more that will be at stake."

"I know," John said.

"And if you need to talk to somebody, give me call—and I'll get your mother." The words hung in the air, taking a moment to register, and then John and his dad broke into laughter.

Chapter Fourteen

John inhaled the clean, sweet night air as they strolled to the car. The afternoon rain had left the air smelling crisp and earthy. The remaining thunderclouds drifted off, and the stars twinkled in the sky like gems on jeweler's velvet.

It was a quiet night, meant for contemplation, but John felt anything but collected. The remarkable conversation with his father and the task at hand flew around in his head like sparrows trapped in a house.

The time had come to tell the truth. He tried to think how best to broach the subject but only drew a blank.

"Are you satisfied?" He unlocked the car.

"With what?" Karyn looked at him.

"That I have parents, that my folks are not wanted by the FBI for heinous crimes against humanity?"

She smiled. "Yeah. Your folks are very nice. Down-to-earth. I don't know why you were so reluctant to have me meet them. I was starting to wonder about your intentions," she said pointedly.

"I haven't met *your* mother," he shot back.

"*My* mother lives a thousand miles away in another state."

John helped Karyn into the car, rounded the vehicle and took the driver's seat. "I hope my mom didn't grill you too badly. She's been waiting years for this moment." He started the engine.

"This moment?"

"When I brought someone home to meet her."

"You don't bring your girlfriends to meet your parents?"

"Not since high school." He checked his mirrors before pulling out.

"You're kidding. Why not?"

"There's never been anyone special before."

Her hand sought his on the steering wheel and squeezed. "Thank you. You mean a lot to me, too."

"I hope so."

He *really* hoped so—hoped the strength of her feelings would be enough for her to forgive him and accept what he did.

He started the engine. "You were right about my dad and me," he said, to make conversation. "You're very good at getting to the heart of relationships."

"I'll send you my bill. I noticed you seemed to be getting along better after dinner. I heard you two laughing as your mom and I were doing the dishes."

"Yeah. Dad and I had a little talk. Cleared the air." John took a deep breath. "You and I need to talk." The words thudded in his chest, and he risked a glance at her face.

"I've told you before that what happened before we met doesn't matter. It's only from this point forward that counts." She touched his arm.

"My grandmother says the past influences the future."

"It certainly makes us what we are," she agreed, not noticing that he'd spoken of grandmother in the present tense.

* * *

John waited while Karyn switched on the lights. Around his ankles, Suki the cat twined. Over time, the cat had forgiven him for Stanley's transgressions. He hoped that Karyn would be as forgiving.

"Would you like a drink?" Karyn asked.

"That would be great." He'd take his courage wherever he could find it.

"Wine or something stronger?"

"Scotch would be great. Ice. A little water."

John moved to the sofa and sank into its cushions, feeling almost weak-kneed.

One of those padded, elaborately frilled photo albums that women seemed to be so fond of rested on Karyn's coffee table. To quell his jittering nerves, he flipped through the album as he waited for Karyn to return with his drink. He recognized pictures of her at a birthday party, with a guy he supposed was her ex-fiancé, and with an older woman he immediately recognized by the resemblance as her mother.

As he turned the pages, the frenetic, jitterbugging of his nerves subsided to a slow waltz, and he began to enjoy the photographic glimpse into Karyn's life.

Christmas with her mother and brother. A day spent in Port Townsend. Watching the fish fly at Pike Place market downtown.

The last page struck him like an electric shock to the chest.

The tinkling of ice in a glass signaled Karyn had returned. She handed him the scotch, and he took a gulp. It burned his throat, but did nothing to release the weight that pressed against him.

Karyn glanced at the photograph on the open page. "That's my friend Celine Dufresne."

"You and Celine are friends?" he choked on the words.

"You know her?" Karyn's eyebrows arched

"She looks familiar," he evaded. "What does Celine do for a living?"

"She's a police officer."

"Have you known her long?"

"Since I moved to Seattle. I've been meaning to have you meet her. She's the closest thing to family I have in Seattle. I've told her all about you."

"You have?" To his own ears, his voice sounded like he had laryngitis.

"Why wouldn't I? She's anxious to meet you."

John downed the remainder of his drink, then choked as the scotch went down the wrong pipe. Karyn thumped him on the back. "Are you all right?"

"What did you tell her?" he squeaked.

Karyn shrugged. "The basics. Age, general physical description, occupation. First name. I didn't tell her anymore, because she wanted to run you through the computer at the station—are you okay? You don't look good."

He didn't feel good. "I'm okay."

"Celine is the one who put the ad in the classifieds."

John forced himself to breathe normally. Obviously, Celine hadn't made the connection between John, Karyn's friend, and the guy she'd been investigating.

Yet.

"We have to get together soon," Karyn said. "Maybe meet for a drink after work?"

"So she can check me out?" He forced a laugh.

Karyn wrapped her arms around him. "I promise

I won't let her frisk you. Now what is it you want to talk to me about?"

John closed the photo album so Celine's face wouldn't stare at him, mock him.

"You've worked in hospitals," he said. "Have you worked with patients who died on the operating table and then came back to life?"

"Near death experiences." She nodded. "I've only actually worked with one case. It's a hallucination thing, caused by chemicals released in the brain."

"That's what you believe?"

"That's the scientific explanation."

"Why is it then that so many people seem to have a similar experience—the bright light, the tunnel, the astral travel aspect of feeling like they've left their bodies?"

"I guess because chemicals are drugs that affect the human body in similar ways."

Not a good beginning.

But he had no choice but to trudge forward, through the waist-deep mire his deceit had caused. Some day Celine and Karyn would share the right notes to enable Celine to make the connection. And besides that, he had his future to consider. What if the relationship turned into something permanent? He couldn't lie about his occupation for the rest of his life.

"I've had near death experiences."

"You have?" Her eyes grew round.

"I died when I was six years old," he said quietly. "My folks found me in my room. Dead. My dad did CPR, the whole bit. It changed my life."

"I would imagine so." She touched his knee in a gesture intending to comfort. "That must have been horrible. And your poor parents! My God. What happened?"

John took a deep breath. "I wanted to see my grandmother, and she was dead. I simply . . . drifted over to the Other Side. One second I was on earth, and then a tunnel, filled with light like you can't imagine, opened up. Karyn, there's a whole world out there! Not a world, a universe, an existence that's impossible to describe."

"You must have been ill or something. Hallucinating. It's very common when children get high fevers." Her practical explanation hit him hard.

John shook his head. "My heart stopped, my breathing stopped."

"John, people just don't die. That's the thing about hallucinations—people believe what they're seeing is real."

Again he shook his head and insisted, "I watched the whole thing—saw myself lying on the floor, my father performing CPR. And I knew I didn't have to go back, but my grandmother told me I should."

"That's all part of the hallucination. Renowned doctors, experts in psychiatry and neurology, have studied near death experiences. When the brain is deprived of oxygen or is chemically stressed, it does weird things. It hallucinates."

"Karyn." John steeled his courage. "I can still do it."

"Do what?"

"Die and come back." His words were barely above a whisper but they seemed to echo in the room.

She laughed.

He didn't know what he had expected, but laughter wasn't it. "I'm not kidding."

"Come on."

"I'm not kidding," he insisted.

"You're still having near death experiences?" She cocked her head, uncertain whether he was joking.

He nodded.

"Have you seen a doctor?"

"I don't need one."

"John, if your heart stops, that's serious. You can't ignore it and hope it will go away." She stared at him. "I know an excellent doctor, a cardiologist. I'll get his number . . ." She jumped up and would have gone to get her address book, but John caught her hand, and turned her around to face him.

"No. That's not what I want. Wait, Karyn. Wait."

Karyn looked at him expectantly.

"I don't want to correct the problem. It's not a problem." Except of course in his personal life.

"It's not a problem? How can you say that?" Hands on her hips, she stared at him.

"It's not dangerous," he argued futilely. His great confession had become a medical problem to be biopsied, treated, cured.

"How often does it occur?" She sank on the sofa, her knees touching his.

"Whenever I want it to."

"Why would you want it to?"

How else am I going to get messages to people who've died? he wanted to say. That would go over big. She just about had him scheduled with a cardiologist. If he said any more, she'd have him committed to the mental ward.

"Let's just forget I said anything."

Her fingers brushed the hair off her face. "I don't understand why you won't have this problem taken care of. Are you afraid of what the doctors might discover? Are you warning me, in case we're in the middle of dinner and you suddenly keel over?"

"That's not going to happen."

"How do you know?"

"I just do."

"You can't control something like this any more than an epileptic can control his seizures without medication."

John set his now empty drink on the coffee table. "I'm sorry."

"For what?"

For botching the confession. For the misunderstanding. For lying. For everything.

"I don't know," he said. "For dragging you into this."

"You don't have anything to be sorry about, but you do have to get this checked."

John leaned close and kissed her lightly. "I'd better go."

"I worry about you." She hugged him tight.

"I know. And I know I can't convince you, but you don't need to worry about me."

He removed her arms from around his neck, clasped her hand between his, and lightly kissed her fingers. "I'd better go. This didn't work out the way I expected."

"What did you expect?"

Anger. Disappointment. Tears. Anything but a medical diagnosis.

Chapter
Fifteen

John foresaw two possible outcomes when Karyn learned the complete truth: She'd think he was the world's biggest fraud or the world's biggest nutcase. Either way, he was destined to lose.

As the pendulum of doom swung over his head, John tried to find a way out his dilemma. He grappled with it for days, but the solution eluded him. In fact, the only thing that solidified was his feelings for Karyn. He missed her tremendously.

He phoned, but only her machine answered his call. After she failed to return several calls, paranoia hatched, and he began to suspect that she was deliberately avoiding him. Did she not know how to respond to his confession or did she decide she didn't want to see him anymore? Then again, maybe Celine finally lowered the boom.

As time passed without a return call, his anxiety grew.

* * *

The hospital operator connected him and the phone rang on the other end. Once. Twice. Three times. Four. Five. Six. Doesn't anybody work there? he wondered, tapping on the desk. On the seventh ring, it was answered. "Medical Social Services," said the female voice.

"May I speak to Karyn Walker, please?" John forced a polite tone.

"She's not in today." The distracted tone said don't bother me, I'm busy. Papers rustled in the background, sounding like dry autumn leaves crunching underfoot.

"Do you know when she'll be back?" John suppressed his impatience.

"No, I don't."

"Is there someone who does? It's important."

The woman sighed heavily. "Just a minute." He heard her ask, "Janie, do you know when Karyn will be back?" but was unable to catch the response.

"Thursday," the woman said when she came back to the phone.

"Is she sick?"

"I don't know."

He kept a firm hold on his temper, as if it were a wild animal that he didn't dare let loose. "Could you find out, please?"

"Who is this?" She sounded annoyed.

"This is Doctor Metcalf."

Instantly, she was cooperative. "Oh, Dr. Metcalf, I'm sorry. One moment, please." A few seconds later she came back on the line. "Miss Walker is attending a social services conference in San Francisco. She'll be back Thursday."

A conference? Karyn had left on a conference and not even bothered to tell him she was going? They didn't account for every second of their time with each other, but an out-of-town business trip would seem to warrant at least a mention over dinner.

"Thank you," John said tightly.

"You're welcome, Doctor."

John slammed the phone into the cradle, his

anger catching fire like a match to old newspaper. "Damn it!"

* * *

The life force moved sluggishly through miles of vessels; his heart rate slowed. Long minutes stretched between breaths. An electrical charge flowed over him; the air seemed to sizzle. Finally, his heart ceased pumping and, moments later, one last shuddering breath rattled through his body. His soul slipped free.

The tunnel opened and he floated through the crystal light to the Other Side.

As usual, his grandmother wasted no time on preliminaries. "Been having a few problems, huh?"

"I tried to tell Karyn the truth. She thinks I have a medical condition that needs to be cured. Once we got on that I got sidetracked and didn't have a chance to tell her the rest."

"Didn't have a chance? Or didn't take it?"

"How could I have told her? She thinks I'm crazy."

"She doesn't think you're crazy."

"She went out of town and didn't tell me."

"And after you told her about coming here, didn't you feel like you needed space to regroup?"

"So?"

"So maybe she needed the same thing. Or got called away unexpectedly."

"It's not fair!" A spate of anger surged through him, rippling through the mist.

"That she didn't call you?"

"That everything should be so difficult. That I should meet someone who doesn't understand or won't accept what I do."

"John, you chose to do what you do. You said as much to Karyn. And you chose her. You answered the ad. You lied about what you do, and you continued to pursue her even after you had a good idea how she would feel. Don't blame some cosmic unfairness for the state you're in."

Annoyance and acceptance warred within him.

"I could give this all up," he mused.

"Could you?"

"It would make my life easier. There'd be no more undercover investigations, Dad would have a normal son. Karyn would be happier."

As John envisioned his life without the Other Side, a yawning void opened before him, and a wind of melancholy swept through his being, chilling him to the soul.

"No," he admitted. "I can't give it up. It's a part of me. To sever the connection to the Other Side would be cutting off a part of myself." He sighed. "But Karyn will never accept this and I couldn't stand to lose her either. So what's the answer?"

"Johnny," his grandmother said sadly, "I can't tell you. I have to let things play out the way they're meant to be. The answer is out there, but you have to find it."

"But what if I don't?"

"The answer is in the quest, Johnny, not in the final answer."

* * *

John visited with his grandmother for a while longer, then readied himself to return. Before he could leave, he sensed a revenant radiating a summons.

"Mrs. Boswell!" he gasped.

"Mr. Metcalf. So nice to see you again." She was as formal as ever.

"You're dead!" He stated the obvious.

"Never felt better," she said. "I'm finally reunited with dear Montague." As she spoke, John became aware of her husband's presence.

"She hasn't changed a bit. She's still the same girl who lit my campfire." Mr. Boswell glowed with emotion.

Mrs. Boswell giggled.

"You have an appointment to see me next week," he protested, still dazed.

"You'd better cancel that, young man. I'm not going to be able to make it," she tittered.

"What happened?" John was still stunned.

"I passed on in my sleep. It's the best way to go," she explained.

"One minute she was snorin' away . . ." Mr. Boswell began.

"I beg your pardon, Monague, but I do not snore. I was quietly sleeping when the good Lord decided it was time for me to journey to my final destination. And here I am."

"You're right, dear," Mr. Boswell apologized. "I was teasing you."

"You, young man, should have told me you don't like prune strudel. That goes for you, as well, Montague," she scolded.

"I didn't want to hurt your feelings," John said lamely, as Mr. Boswell nodded his agreement.

"I understand you meant well," she conceded. Then, as wonderment filled the mist, she said, "I must say He isn't anything like what I expected," she said.

"Who?" John asked.

"God," she answered. "Aren't all those Fundamentalists going to be surprised!" She chuckled in delight. "I can hardly wait."

"I notice you said 'He'" John said. "Does that mean that God is male?" Because he was on a traveler's visa and not an actual citizen of the Other Side, John had never met God.

"No," she said. "Just that there's no pronoun to describe God in a way that you'd understand."

"You just have to be here," Mr. Boswell said. "Be a part of it."

"Exactly," she affirmed. "I'm just so grateful that I was able to connect with my dear Montague through you, young man. I want to thank you for your assistance."

"You're welcome."

"I'm going to miss you," she said.

"I'll be seeing you here," John pointed out.

An electrical current of some emotion passed through Mrs. Boswell, but was quickly masked. Too fleeting to define, it nevertheless kindled an unease in John.

"Well," she said. "I know how busy you are, and how many things you have to do. I just want you know that I wish you all the best, and I want to thank you for everything you've done for me."

"I come here all the time."

"Well, if I don't see you, I want you to know that I'm thinking of you and wish you well. And, I suppose I'll see you soon enough. Good luck to you, young man. And to your young lady. You two will live a long and happy life together."

She knew about Karyn? Or was she speaking about someone else? He wanted to ask her questions, but she began to fade away.

"I'd better run," she said. "Montague and I have a

lot of catching up to do, and I have a lot of old friends to look up."

With the departure of the Boswells, John grew pensive. Did everyone around him know what was going to happen except him? It was so frustrating. What he needed was a *Life Instruction Manual* to help him put the pieces together in the correct sequence since some assembly did seem to be required. And, right now, John suspected his box was missing a few key parts.

The only thing he was sure of was that he didn't want to lose Karyn and he couldn't give up his travels to the Other Side.

Chapter Sixteen

Just when he had stopped hoping that every phone call might be from Karyn, she called.

"I wasn't ignoring you," she said without preamble. "I was out of town."

"I know. When I couldn't reach you. I called you at work."

"It was a sudden thing. One of the other social workers was signed up to go and she had to cancel at the last minute, so I went in her place. I tried to call you. If I had your work number, I would have called you there," she said.

"Why didn't you leave a message on my machine?"

"I never got a machine. Your phone just rang and rang."

John eyed the answering machine. For the first time he noticed the light was out that indicated the machine was switched on. No wonder she couldn't reach him.

"I must have bumped it or something. The machine's been off."

"I knew you'd be wondering what had happened to me, but I had no way to reach you."

"I was getting worried. After our discussion the other night, I was afraid of what you might think."

"I'm sorry. I know my reaction wasn't what you expected," she said. "I've just never heard of anything like that. I've heard of near death experiences, of course, but never of anyone trying to bring one on at will and being successful at it."

"It's a lot to take in," he agreed. "This isn't the first time it's caused a problem in my life."

"I don't want it to be a problem."

"Me either," he said. Holding the receiver against his ear, he lifted the phone from the counter and slid to the floor. Back against the wall, he settled in.

"I don't know why I was so—I don't know—flummoxed, I guess," she said.

"Flummoxed?"

"Flummoxed."

He heard amusement in her voice, but her next words were spoken soberly. "I feel we're starting to have something special. Later, after you left, I started to get mad, because I thought you should have told me sooner. But then I asked myself when, and I admit that I couldn't think of the right time. I guess there is no right time for something like this."

Though she didn't know it, she was offering him a lead-in for him to tell her the rest. John opened his mouth, but the words stuck got stuck, like a bitter-tasting pill that lodged in his throat.

He coughed. "How was the conference?"

"Good. It was the annual social workers' association convention.

"So they had seminars and speakers . . ."

"Yeah," Karen affirmed.

"And a keynote address?"

"That was actually pretty interesting. The woman spoke about the changes in the health care industry and how that will affect the medical social work field."

"Did they serve warm rubber chicken for lunch?"

"Cold rubber chicken salad," she said.

"My favorite."

"Sherbet for dessert?" he asked.

"Rainbow," she answered. "I'd like to see you," she said. "I missed you."

"I missed you, too. Do you want to grab a bite to eat?"

"Have you ever been to The Steak Out? People at work said it was pretty good," she suggested.

The infamous Steak Out, where he had caught Reid in an extramarital luncheon rendezvous? "I've been there once or twice."

* * *

This is where I belong.

The unbidden sentiment popped into his mind as he enveloped Karyn into a hug. "You feel good to me," he said softly.

Karyn had met him at door before he could even knock, a welcoming smile on her face that he couldn't help but respond to. A simple red T-shirt dress clung in all the right places without being too obvious. The brightness of the fabric brought out the color in her face. Her hair curled around her cheeks, looking soft and touchable.

"I missed you. I'm sorry I didn't try harder to reach you when I left." She hugged him back.

"That's okay. I understand. It was my fault."

"Thank you. Are you ready to go, or would you like to have a drink and relax for a minute?" she asked.

If he had the drink, they'd never make it out the front door. That wasn't a bad thing, except that they had unfinished business. He tried to imagine how good it would feel once everything was out in the open and he didn't have to worry about letting something slip, about someone else letting something slip.

Actually, he didn't know how that would feel. He had been hiding what he did for so long, secrecy had become normal to him.

He was still standing in the foyer; the front door was wide open. Should he stay or should they go? Inside or outside. Truth or Dare. "Why don't we have a drink at the restaurant?" John decided. "I called and made reservations."

"So did I," she said.

"We shouldn't have trouble getting a seat, then."

* * *

"I'll let you out and go park the car," John offered as they circled The Steak Out for the third time. The place was packed. There wasn't a single space available in the entire parking lot.

"I can't believe this," Karyn said. "It's a week night. Why aren't all these people home watching TV?"

"*News Flash?*" John quipped, thinking of his father.

"Yeah." She smiled. "Just park anywhere. I'll walk with you."

He found a place on the street a block away. Though Seattle was often rainy, but the weather had been clear lately, and the stars sparkled in a cloud-free sky. The air was warm and caressing and charged with potential. It was the kind of evening that made John feel like anything was possible.

Or maybe it was the fact that Karyn strolled along at his side.

He stretched an arm across her shoulders, hers curved around his waist. Their steps fell into a rhythm. He gave a quick kiss to her hair, just above her ear.

"I'm glad you're here," he said.

She smiled. "I thought about you the whole time I was at the conference."

"Are you sure it wasn't indigestion from the rubber chicken?" he joked.

They walked a few paces in silence. "I love Seattle," she said. "It's a beautiful city. It reminds me of San Francisco, only cleaner."

"I've lived here all my life," he said.

"You've never wanted to go anyplace else?"

He had no urge to travel since he'd made the ultimate journey and had gone as far as anyone could go. "And leave such a beautiful, clean San Francisco-esque city?" he answered.

"You've got a point," she said.

The restaurant was dimly lit, and it took a moment for John's eyes to adjust. When they did, he saw that, as the parking lot had hinted, the place was filled to capacity, with standing room only in the waiting area. A crowd of impatient people swarmed around a podium guarded by a harried hostess.

It took a while, but when they reached the podium, they were seated immediately.

"Got any plans for this weekend?" John asked after they were shown to a table. "My sister is having a get-together. A backyard barbecue and a little hot tubbing this Saturday night. Do you want to go?"

Initially when Sandy had invited him, he had declined, still upset over Reid's extramarital affair.

It might have been the spell of evening or maybe Karyn's presence, but it didn't sound like such a bad idea anymore. Though he'd told Sandy no, he didn't foresee a problem in changing his mind.

"Sounds like fun," Karyn said.

"It's a date then." He envisioned them sitting in the hot tub, playing footsies.

"Are we still dating?" she asked.

"What would you call it?"

"Maybe seeing each other." She sipped her wine and regarded him over the rim of her glass.

"I'm not familiar with the nuances. At what point does dating become seeing someone?"

"I think the crossover occurs after you've slept with someone."

"So if you go out, have dinner, give 'em a kiss good night at the door and leave, it's dating."

"Right." She nodded.

"If you go out, have dinner, go home and have hot and sweaty sex, it's seeing someone." It amazed John that women not only thought about these things, but categorized and indexed them.

"It doesn't even have to be hot and sweaty."

"That's certainly cleared up a lot. I guess I've dated a lot more than I thought," John laughed. He leaned forward slightly. She had the sexiest eyes. The candlelight glinted off her hair and made her skin glow. "Did I ever tell you how sexy you are?"

Her brows drew together as if mulling it over. "Was that you?"

"Ha. Ha. Very funny. Just how many men have told you you were sexy?"

She looked around the room. "What did you order that's taking so long?"

"Your order, sir. Madam." The black-suited waiter appeared at their table, a tray balanced on his shoulder.

With flourish, he opened up a stand, set the tray on it and uncovered the dishes. Steam rose, filling the air with a delicious aroma.

"Smells great," Karyn said.

"Thank you," said the waiter proudly, as if he had cooked it himself. With an exaggerated movement, he placed the plates before John and Karyn.

Conversation waned as they became absorbed in their meal, cocooned by the muted conversational hum of the dining crowd. Relieved of the need to converse, John's mind searched for a way to broach the subject of his occupation. He needed to be smooth, careful, to gather information before he divulged his own.

Batter up. "Do you remember the fortune-teller at the carnival?" John placed his silverware horizontally across the top of his plate to signal he'd finished eating.

"The shyster who made money by preying on the gullibility of others?"

Strike one.

"That's the one." John scanned the restaurant for the waiter. "Do you want another drink?"

"No, thank you. Why?"

"I thought you might want another drink." He feigned an interest in a dark blotch on the tablecloth where he'd spilled something.

"I meant, why are you asking about the fortune-teller?" She said patiently and fixed her gaze on him.

It wasn't the opening he had hoped for, but it was an opening. He should make the best of it and seize the opportunity.

"I know the experience your mother and your family had with the psychic wasn't a good one. Was that your only contact with a spiritualist?" he asked as casually as he could with his heart thumping in his chest.

"Wasn't it enough?"

Strike two.

John selected his next words carefully. "There are shady used car salesmen, crooked cops, ambulance-chasing attorneys, but most people in those occupations are decent people. Don't you think that there might be some spiritualists who have supernatural ability?"

"The only ability they have is a knack for conning people."

Strike three.

If this had been a Mariner's game, he'd be out. Fortunately, it was only his life, he thought facetiously, so he had another chance.

"Some might have a genuine desire to help people."

"John, get real." She snorted. "At best they provide light entertainment."

"You've personally never been to one."

"Of course not. Have you?"

Been to one. Been one. Close enough. "As a matter of fact. . .".

Her jaw dropped.

He met her gaze, saying nothing.

"What did she tell you? Did she tell you a tall blond woman would come into your life?" Karyn asked sarcastically.

"He."

"A tall blond man was supposed to come into your life?"

"No. The psychic was a he."

"So what did he tell you?"

"I learned my grandmother was happy in the afterlife. That there is an afterlife, but that the life we're living now is just as important."

"And you believe that?" her eyebrows arched.

"Should I believe that my grandmother is unhappy? Or that she died and exists no more? Or do you mean that once we die, all trace of our existence is erased?"

"You're twisting my words around. That there is an afterlife, and the fact that your grandmother is there is a matter of faith. It doesn't take a fortune-teller to tell you that. I could have told you that and saved you few bucks."

"But you would have been guessing. He was very specific. He knew things about my grandmother that only I knew."

"It may have seemed that way, but he probably picked up cues from you. They fish around and when they hit on something that's true, you react in such a way that they know they've struck a nerve. What surprises me is that you felt you needed to see a psychic."

"Why?"

"Your near death experience hallucinations. Most people who have them are convinced of the afterlife."

It did convince me, Karyn, and that's why I'm using it to help other people. That's all he needed to say. But somehow the words wouldn't come.

"So you don't believe in near death experiences, but you believe in the afterlife?" he asked. "Isn't that a contradiction?"

"John, when you die, you die. There's no coming back to earth."

"That doesn't answer my question."

"Yes, I believe in an afterlife. I mean, I have to. Otherwise, what's the point of life at all?"

"I don't understand how you can assign everything into neat compartments. This is true. This isn't true. Why are near death experiences more incredible than an afterlife?"

Karyn rubbed her temples. "You're making my head hurt. John, I don't have all the answers. I know you were affected by the experience you had as a child. It was very powerful. I didn't have that experience. I'm coming from the viewpoint of a clinician. She reached across the table and clasped his hand. "I don't see us arriving at a solution tonight. Please, can we talk about something else?"

He returned the squeeze. He agreed with Karyn's summation that they would not arrive at a solution. Perhaps it was enough that they were at least able to talk about it. It was a beginning.

The waiter dropped by the table to ask if they needed anything, and John requested the check.

"Should we bring anything to your sister's?" Karyn asked.

"I'll grab a bottle of wine. Dress casual and bring your swimsuit."

They left the restaurant, went back to Karyn's house, and had hot and sweaty sex.

"You're right," John said afterwards. "This definitely isn't dating."

Chapter Seventeen

John glowered at his brother-in-law and felt a heat rise in him that owed nothing to the temperature of the water in the spa. He itched to grab the SOB and hold his head underwater.

And the bimbo.

Hello again, I'm Caitlin Mitchell. Reid's associate. Remember we met at The Steak Out?

He remembered all right. What he couldn't recall was exactly what he'd uttered after he and Karyn followed Sandy out to the patio and found Reid, Caitlin, and Caitlin's "date," Dave, soaking in the hot tub. The apoplectic rage had erased everything but the seething anger that simmered like a pot of hot stew beneath his façade of control.

After joining the group in the spa for a while, Sandy had excused herself and returned to the house to check on dinner. Dave had followed, offering to help.

John also had volunteered, but she'd waved him aside, saying that with Dave's help she had it under control. Her refusal of his offer brought a measure of relief. It was silly, but he didn't want to leave Reid and Caitlin alone.

Karyn would be there, but he couldn't very well request that she baby-sit his brother-in-law and the "associate." He scowled at the couple sitting across from him, but they took no notice. Watching them sitting together, sipping wine coolers, speaking in low tones swallowed by the sound of Jacuzzi jets, raised his temperature more than a few degrees.

"Is something wrong? You haven't said two words since we got here. Are you all right?" Karyn studied his face.

"I'm fine."

"Are you mad about something?"

Hell yes, he was mad about something. But not at Karyn. "No, just a little preoccupied. Sorry." He tried to soften the terseness in his tone. He shifted his gaze from the couple opposite him and turned to Karyn.

She had pinned up her hair, and the steam from the water caused it to curl into little ringlets. Her face turned a becoming pink from the heat of the water.

"I'm a terrible date," he said. "I invite you to spend the day with me, then I ignore you."

"I don't feel ignored. I just sense that something is wrong," she said, cupping her hands together and letting the water run through her fingers. He watched, distracted for the moment from his obsession.

"Hey." He leaned close. She raised her head, and he kissed her lightly. Through the steam of the spa, he could feel the warmth of her breath caressing his face.

"Hey, hey. None of that! This is a family spa, you know." Across from them, Reid sat, near enough to touch Caitlin, but not so near as to draw attention. Reid was being circumspect, if bringing one's lover home to meet the wife could be said to be discreet at all.

Caitlin's behavior was something else. Her lips bore a perpetual sly smile, as if she alone enjoyed an inside joke.

John glared at Reid and watched in satisfaction as his smile faltered. "Why don't you eat sh—" John's biting comment was cut short by Karyn's gasp.

"John, he's kidding. What's wrong with you?" She gaped at him.

"I guess I need to cool off. Can I get you anything Karyn?" John leaped out of the spa, splashing water onto the terra-cotta patio tiles.

"A wine cooler. Do you need any help?"

"I think I can manage a wine cooler. I'll be right back. Stay and keep Reid and Caitlin company." John grabbed a towel off a nearby patio chair and headed inside.

"What do you have to drink around this place?" He forced cheerfulness into his voice as he entered the kitchen.

Sandy stood at the sink chopping vegetables, using a technique that mirrored their mother's, but her actions appeared mechanical as if her mind were elsewhere.

She jumped as John let the kitchen door slam.

"You scared me!" she said.

"Where's our boy Dave?" John surveyed the area for Caitlin's date.

"He decided candles would be romantic after dark, so he went to get some."

"Uh huh."

"He's very nice." Sandy diced bell pepper.

"Did you know that you make salad just like Mom?"

"I do not." She shot him a look of annoyance over her shoulder.

"Yes, you do. You cut things into microscopic pieces like she does." John laughed and stole a tomato bit from the salad.

Sandy slapped at his hand. "Stop that. There's beer and wine in the fridge. And some wine coolers. Reid made a pitcher of Margaritas."

"I'll have a beer." John scanned the labels. Foreign brands predominated, with nary a domestic light. He selected the least imposing beer, the one with a name he could pronounce.

After several wrong picks, he found the right drawer with the bottle opener. "You have an unusual a selection of beer," he said.

"Reid likes foreign beers. He says American beer tastes like watered cat piss."

"It's good that a man can have a hobby." John kept his tone light.

"He's been playing racquetball and golfing a lot lately." She tossed the salad with a large wooden fork and spoon. "Caitlin is friendly, don't you think?"

As friendly as a bitch in heat. "Uh huh." John took a slug of the strong, full-bodied brew.

"Is it my imagination or does Dave seem a little— never mind. It's none of my business." Sandy stowed the salad in the refrigerator and began cleaning up.

"Gay?"

"I shouldn't talk about him. He's very sweet." She wiped the counter.

John crossed his ankles, leaning back against the stove. He took another swig of the beer. It really wasn't bad.

"I got the impression he and Caitlin have been friends a while. They go out quite a bit together," Sandy said.

"There's nothing wrong with that." John examined the label on the bottle. The alcohol content indicated it was quite a hearty brew.

"She's very pretty. I'm sure she could attract any man she wanted," Sandy said. "Dave doesn't seem like her type."

"Especially if he's gay," John added wryly.

Sandy took a deep breath. "I've been debating whether to ask you—there isn't anyone else I feel I can trust—"

The muscles in his face froze as if rigor mortis had suddenly set in.

"Reid and I—"

Oh crap, Sandy. Don't ask me about Reid and Caitlin. "—are going away next weekend. My sitter's son has the chicken pox, Reid's folks are out of town, Mom has one of her sorority functions . . . could you watch the kids for us?"

"I'd love to," he croaked, his mouth dry. He took a long drink of beer.

"You would?" She raised her eyebrows.

"You *know* how much I adore my little niece and nephew."

"I know you like them in small, supervised doses."

"Sandy, Sandy, Sandy." He put his arm around his sister's shoulders and squeezed. "Have I ever found anything but joy in the company of my beloved sister's offspring?"

"What's the catch?" She eyed him.

"No catch!" John held up his hands. "You and Reid go and have a great time wherever you're going. The kids are on solid food now, right?"

She shot him a look. "Very funny," she said. Then, seriously, "Thank you. We haven't been away in a long time. Reid's gone so much these days."

"Don't worry about the kids. We'll do fine. Where are the little rug rats by the way?"

"Now you make me wonder about your ability to baby-sit—you've been here an hour and you've just started to wonder where the kids are?"

"I couldn't concentrate with all the silence. Besides," he wrapped his arm around his sister again, "that was before I knew I was going to have the responsibility."

"They're at Mom's." She ducked under his arm. A rustling drew their attention to the door. "I'm back! Did you miss me?" Dave held a politically correct cloth shopping bag.

He was a small guy, no more than five foot six or so, but well-muscled as a result of daily body-building workouts at the gym. His arms and legs looked baby smooth, leading John to assume he shaved more than his face. Dave seemed affable, likeable and easy-to-please. And, as Sandy had noticed herself, unsuitable for Caitlin.

Sandy eyed the bag. "You must have a lot of candles."

Dave giggled. "I found some lovely Chinese lanterns I thought would be perfect. You don't mind, do you?"

"Go right ahead. Decorating is not my forte," Sandy answered.

"Then I'll get started." With a little jump of excitement, Dave headed outside.

"Caitlin and Dave . . ." John mused as the door swung shut with a click.

"No way!" He and Sandy spoke at once. They laughed.

"Are you about finished in here?" John asked. "Why don't you come outside and join the party?"

"I have a few more things to do. Then I'll come out. You go on."

John remembered Karyn waited for him and a wine cooler. "I'll grab another beer and a cooler for Karyn, then."

He opened the refrigerator. "That's the trouble with being a host. You throw a party and you don't have the time to spend with the guests. If they want to talk to you they have to go to the kitchen."

"I don't mind," Sandy said. "But this is actually Reid's party. He suggested we invite Caitlin and her 'beau' over for dinner. I suggested we barbecue and invite you and Karyn."

John hit his head on a rack in the refrigerator. He turned to look at his sister. "Reid wanted to invite Caitlin to dinner? Here?"

"Yes." Sandy nodded. She didn't appear to be concerned.

"You're kidding!"

The clatter of pots and pans she had been unloading from the dishwasher stopped. He had her attention. "When we first got married, he invited people for dinner all the time. Mostly senior execs of the company who he wanted to impress. Sometimes just friends.

"We used to have a lot of fun," Sandy mused. "You get so caught up in the day-to-day business, you don't realize that time is passing and you're drifting apart. One day you look up and you're here and he's way over there. It's like you're in two different rowboats paddling alongside each other. You both stop to attend to something and the next thing you know the current has separated you." Her expression was sad.

"Then you have to row like hell to get back together," John said.

She nodded.

Unfortunately, a wave could hit at any moment and drive them farther apart or even capsize the boat. Sandy, while aware things weren't the way they used to be, was oblivious to the approaching tidal wave.

"Sometimes I look at our lives and I wonder what happened. It's like that Carpenter's song, "We've Only Just Begun." We started out with so many hopes. Nothing was settled, nothing was for sure, everything was uncertain. But we shared our hopes. Do you know what I mean?" Sandy looked at him intently.

John nodded.

"And he was fun. Romantic. Silly. Now he shows more attention to his coworkers than he does me."

John reread the label on his beer bottle.

His sister leaned against the counter. "All I wanted was to have a happy family and become a moderately successful attorney. From the outside looking in, it appears as if I've accomplished that, but you know what? I never got to the happy part."

John placed his beer on the counter and wrapped an arm around his sister's shoulder. "Everything works out as it should," he said, aware his words held veracity if no comfort.

"I know." She pulled away and John noticed her eyes glinted with unshed tears. "I'm looking at this weekend with Reid as a new beginning. I know we won't resolve everything, but I think it will be a start."

"Where are you going?" John asked. He hoped his sister was right, but given the way Reid was carrying on with Caitlin, a romantic getaway seemed incomprehensible.

"To a little bed and breakfast on the coast."

"There you are!" Karyn stepped into the kitchen, a towel wrapped sarong style around her waist. "Did you get lost? What happened to my wine cooler?"

"I waylaid him," Sandy said, "It's my fault. What kind of cooler would you like? Berry, berry light or citrus?"

"Citrus," Karyn answered.

Sandy handed her a cooler, and then said, "I'm going outside to join the party. Come on out when you're ready."

"Is something wrong?" Karyn asked after Sandy left.

John hesitated, unsure how much to reveal. "Sandy has been feeling a little estranged from Reid lately."

"I see." Her tone implied more than her words revealed.

"What does that mean?" John asked.

"It's probably nothing. I shouldn't even say anything. It was probably an accident."

John's eyes narrowed. "What?"

"With all the bubbles, you can't see below the surface and if you move, you bump into people. At first I thought Reid was trying to play footsies with me," she said.

"What?!" John gripped the beer bottle so hard, his knuckles turned white.

"But it wasn't me he was searching for. He was playing footsies with Caitlin."

Relief washed over him like the tide splashing on the beach, then receded and left embarrassment on his sister's behalf.

"You knew." Karyn peered at him, correctly interpreting his silence. "That's what's been bugging you since we got here."

John nodded. "But Sandy doesn't know."

"Haven't you told her?"

"Would you? If she were your sister?"

"Of course I would," she avowed. "No. Maybe. I don't know!" She reversed herself. "How long have Sandy and Reid been married?"

"Ten years." John took a swig of his beer.

"He has a lot of nerve. I take it Dave is just a front."

"I think so."

* * *

Back outside, Reid was swimming laps in the pool. Caitlin was stretched out on a lounge chair; she had slipped the straps of her minute bikini from her shoulders, revealing a back free of tan lines.

Dave and Sandy sat in the spa. He was sharing a remodeling horror story. "And then he said he'd be back in a few hours to finish the cabinets and he never showed up," Dave was saying. "There was dust everywhere! Oh it was dreadful! It made Blue sneeze."

"Blue?" Karyn asked.

"My Blue Persian," Dave replied.

"A Blue Persian named Blue." John figured it out.

"Blue Persians are actually gray, you know," Dave explained. "Her full name is Monique Nicole Bluett. I call her Blue for short. She's won several awards in cat shows," he boasted.

"She sounds lovely," Karyn said.

"She sounds like excellent Doberman bait," Caitlin purred viciously, sitting up and holding her top against her.

"Is that any way to talk to your date?" John baited her.

"Davie knows I'm kidding, don't you?" she asked smoothly.

"You hate her," Dave said. "That's why I don't let you watch her when I go out of town."

John helped Karyn into the spa. Her floral print bikini had a sixties retro look—a full bra and a bottom that came up to her navel—except for the high-cut legs, which made her long legs look even longer.

"Aren't you coming in?" Karyn stood in the Jacuzzi.

John set his beer on the edge of the hot tub. "Just enjoying the view," he said.

Karyn rolled her eyes. "Men."

"Aren't they terrible?" Dave was sympathetic.

John choked back a laugh and Sandy covered her mouth with her hand.

Caitlin retied the bra of her suit and edged into the Jacuzzi. Leaning back, she eased her head onto the padded rest and closed her eyes. "This is wonderful," she said. "You're so lucky." She opened her eyes and looked at Sandy. "If I had a spa, I'd be in it all the time."

"We don't get that much use out of it," Sandy commented. "Mostly when we have people over. It's too cold in winter so we cover it. This is the first time this year we've used it."

"Caitlin's right. We should use it more." Reid climbed into the spa, sitting between Caitlin and his wife.

"Maybe if you were home once in a while, we would." Sharpness edged Sandy's voice.

Reid's eyes narrowed, but he said nothing.

Caitlin shot him a sympathetic glance.

"I'll bet Justin enjoys the pool a lot," Karyn said quickly. "Does he know how to swim?"

"He took lessons last summer," Sandy answered. "But he knows the pool is off limits when we're not around."

"He's such a big boy. I can't believe how much

he's grown," Caitlin said. "And Chelsea's adorable."

John glanced at Reid, who looked like he had swallowed something down the wrong pipe, a tide of red sweeping from neck to hairline.

"When did you meet my kids?" Sandy asked, a puzzled frown settling on her face.

All heads turned toward Caitlin.

"Pictures on my desk," Reid said at the same time that Caitlin answered, "I dropped by here one day to pick up some papers. You were at the store or something."

"Which is it?" Sandy's gaze shifted from Caitlin to Reid and back again.

"She's right," Reid said.

"You must have been very lucky to catch him home." Sandy brushed her hair behind her ears. "You're a lot luckier than I am."

"Anybody hungry? How about if I put the steaks on?" Reid's voice sounded falsely cheerful.

"I'm famished," Dave gushed, oblivious to the tension.

John had never felt less like eating. "I'm starved," he said.

"Me too," Karyn added.

Reid climbed out of the spa and escaped.

* * *

After the party, John and Karyn went to his house. After greeting a boisterous Stanley, by unspoken agreement, they moved into the living room and sank into the sofa.

Karyn spoke slowly, "Well, that was—"

"Awkward," John finished for her. "Sorry. I shouldn't have subjected you to that." Dinner had been uncomfortable, conversation strained, the meal largely untouched. Only Dave had eaten heartily.

"I'm glad you did. It shows that you're willing to share your life with me, warts and all."

"I'm thinking of something stronger that describes Reid, but I'll settle for wart."

"I feel bad for your sister," Karyn said. "She has a lot on her plate—career, kids, problems with Reid."

John sighed. "I know it's tough, but why does she put up with that crap? She's not dumb. My God, she's tried some of the most difficult cases and won. She can put two and two together."

"The spouse is the last to know," Karyn said.

John shook his head. "The spouse is the last to *want* to know. You picked up on it in an afternoon. Sandy knows—she doesn't want to face it. I always thought my sister was stronger than that. Maybe things will work out. She asked me to watch the kids next weekend while she and Reid go away for the weekend. I can see why she'd want to, but I don't understand where he's coming from."

"Just because he's having an affair, doesn't mean he wants a divorce. Some people are never happy with what they have. And their spouses accept that." She shook her head. "I never could. I'd want to know if my husband or boyfriend were cheating on me. I'd want to know so I could dump the bum.

"When you have a relationship of trust and someone lies to you, he's betrayed your trust. If I found out someone I trusted had been lying to me all along, that would be it," she said.

A chill settled in his bones, leaving him feeling nakedly exposed.

"Just like that?" he forced a chuckle "What about extenuating circumstances?"

"What possible extenuating circumstances could there be for lying to someone you loved who trusted you?"

Chapter Eighteen

With a bag of groceries balanced on her hip, Karyn was inserting her key into the lock when the phone rang. Old habits were hard to break; she was still inclined to run for the phone even though she had an answering machine. She fumbled with the key and burst into the house.

Suki twined and Missy danced around her feet, impeding her progress. Karyn tossed the bag on the counter and grabbed the phone.

"Hello?" she panted.

"Sounds like I caught you doing something exciting." Celine sounded amused.

"I just walked in. Hang on a sec." Karyn set the receiver on the counter, closed the front door, and picked up her purse from the entry floor where she'd dropped it.

"I'm back. What's up?" Karyn clamped the phone between her ear and shoulder as she stowed the groceries in the pantry.

"I have an evening free and wondered if you wanted to do anything," Celine said.

"Fine. Like what?"

"That new movie *Expression of Love* is out."

"Is that the one with all the nudity?" Although several of the raciest scenes had been cut, a watchdog group had protested vociferously via media interviews and organized a boycott of the film. The brouhaha meant the film would generate a lot of money for its makers and ensure the male lead instant stardom.

"The photography is supposed to be wonderful," Celine said.

"Since when did you care about photography?"

"Since I have the opportunity to see Stone Thompson in the altogether. And this one won't have subtitles." The last movie they'd seen together had been an incomprehensible foreign film.

"I don't think you need subtitles for 'oh baby,'" Karyn said dryly.

"I'll be over in a little while and we can catch a bite somewhere. The movie starts at eight."

"See you then." Karyn rang off.

Karyn put away the remaining groceries, fed Suki and Missy, and had just changed into more comfortable, casual clothing when Celine arrived. As agreed, they grabbed a couple of fast-food burgers, then went to the movie.

"That wasn't as bad as I thought it was going to be," Karyn said afterward as Celine drove her home.

"Stone Thompson looked pretty good," Celine agreed.

"I meant it had a plot."

"It had a plot?" Celine's eyebrows rose.

"You're one of a kind, Celine."

Celine pulled up to the curb outside Karyn's house. "Coming in?" Karyn asked.

"Yeah. That extra-large Diet Coke I had is starting to do its thing."

"Well, come on then. I'll stay out of your way."

Once inside the house, Celine made a beeline for the bathroom and Karyn picked up Suki and Missy, holding one under each arm. "And how are my girls to night? I've been neglecting you, I know."

Karyn was curled up on the sofa with the dog and cat on her lap when Celine emerged from the bathroom. "There's some wine in the fridge, if you'd like," Karyn offered.

"Thanks. Like a glass?"

"Please."

Celine grinned. "Oh I get it. I'm your waitress tonight."

Celine entered the kitchen, and Karyn could hear her moving about, getting the glasses, opening the refrigerator. She returned to the living room with a glass in each hand, and set Karyn's on the table beside her.

Celine eyed Karyn over the rim of her wineglass. "Still spending a lot of time with what's-his-name?"

"John," Karyn corrected. "And yes I am." She reached for her wine, her head bent, so she couldn't see Celine's face. But she caught the strangled tone of Celine's next words.

"John Metcalf," Celine choked.

"You know him?" Karyn's head shot up. She followed Celine's gaze to the fireplace mantle, where it focused on the old-time photograph taken at the carnival.

Celine moved to the fireplace and picked up the photograph. "Oh, my God, Karyn, this isn't the guy you're seeing?"

"What's wrong?"

"This is John Metcalf." Celine slowly shook her head, as if in a daze, and replaced the photo. Her face had turned a pasty shade of gray. Karyn lifted the dog and cat off her lap and set them on the floor.

"Celine, what's wrong?" Karyn repeated.

Celine didn't answer, but crossed the room to the

sofa and sank into the cushions next to Karyn. "God, Karyn, I'm sorry. I don't know how to tell you this. John Metcalf . . . is the guy we've been investigating."

"Investigating?" Karyn asked unbelievingly. The blood receded from her face in a crawling sensation of fear for John. Was he in trouble?

"He's the psychic."

Karyn could take a joke with the best of them, but she did not see the humor, and this, in fact, bordered on cruel. "That's not funny," she snapped.

Her face a montage of sympathy and dismay, Celine touched Karyn's arm. "I'm not joking." She pointed to the picture on the mantel. "That's the so-called psychic we've been investigating for defrauding his clients."

Karyn shook her head. "You must have him mixed up with somebody else. He just looks like the guy you know. I'm mean, look at his picture. He's behind a costume board! And a gangster costume at that! John is a communications consultant."

"He told you that?"

"Yes." Karyn's head bobbed vigorously.

"Who does he work for?"

"I don't know."

"Where is his office located?"

Karyn bit her lip. "I don't know, exactly."

Scenes replayed themselves in Karyn's mind, like a rented move video on fast forward: John urging her to the fortune-teller booth; his concern that his past would affect their future; and finally, his confession of his near death experiences. The latter clip left a metallic taste in her mouth. It wasn't such a big leap to connect near death experiences to psychic ability. Could John have been trying to package his fortune-telling as near death experiences to make them more palatable?

Like a metastasizing cancer, doubt began to spread, leaving a frosty cold everywhere it touched. "This can't be right. You've got him confused with somebody else. Another John Metcalf. Metcalf isn't an unusual name."

"He owns a gray Ford Explorer, lives on Patterson Street a few blocks from here . . ." Celine rattled off a description that fit John perfectly.

"You're wrong, Celine. Wrong! You have to be. I know him. There's no way this can be true," Karyn argued, although doubt had undermined her conviction. Her belief in his innocence was like a house built on shifting ground—unstable at its very base.

If anyone other than Celine had told her this, Karyn would have rejected it outright. But she trusted Celine.

She trusted John. What reason did he have lie?

How about because he's a charlatan, her inner voice piped up, like a Greek chorus.

Karyn noticed that Celine appeared stricken, looking almost as bad as she, Karyn, felt.

Involuntarily, Karyn's head began to shake from side to side. "I can't deal with this now. It's too much." A part of her, the clinical social worker, stood detached and observed from afar. The social worker part of herself diagnosed that she was probably in shock. "I think I need to be alone," Karyn said in a low voice.

"Karyn, I am so sorry. I'm sorry this happened, and I'm sorry I had to be the one to tell you. Can I get you anything?"

"No. I'll be okay. I just need a little time to think about this." The last thing she wanted to do was think. The second Celine left, she was going to crawl into bed, pull the covers over her head and try to forget this night ever occurred. Somewhere in the back of her mind, she realized she ought to call John, to hear his side of the story, but she didn't have the strength to deal with it. Her fragile composure would not withstand a confrontation. "Okay." Celine patted her hand. "If there's anything I can do, anything at all, please call me."

Her head bowed, Karyn heard, rather than saw, Celine retrieve her purse from the hall tree. Moments later, Celine tucked a piece of paper into Karyn's hand.

"I know you're not ready for this now. But here's his business address. The sign over his office says "Spiritual Advisor." It's on First Street, between Seaport and Main. It's next door to a tattoo parlor."

And Celine left, closing the door quietly.

Chapter Nineteen

Clink.

Was that the doorbell? John strained to hear, but all he picked up was the sound of his own exaggerated breathing. As a sensation of being watched caused the hairs on the back of his neck to raise up, John cracked an eye and stole a peak at his client. Staci Sinclair had her eyes closed. He shook off the feeling and resumed the session.

He still had at least a few minutes of "convergence" with his client's late business partner before he could rouse himself. Think of something else, he told himself. Ignore the itch.

Karyn. He suppressed a smile. It had been a couple of days since he'd seen her. The fact that they were able to speak about his near death experiences filled him with hope that some day soon he'd be able to tell her the whole truth. His client's hands twitched, bringing his focus back to her.

Staci Sinclair's hands felt soft, delicate, the bones fragile underneath the skin. But she was nervous. Her palms were a bit sweaty and shook slightly. She felt uneasy contacting the dead, she had said. It wasn't right. The words "Rest in Peace" were supposed to mean something.

But Staci had to know the truth about her business partner and long-time friend, Janie Alexander, who had died. While Staci had been the creative partner—the one who traveled around the world, selecting the native jewelry they would sell—Janie had handled all the business aspects of their import jewelry business. Over the years, the business that had begun with catalog sales had expanded to a small store. They were going to open a second story when, inexplicably, Janie committed suicide.

Soon after the funeral, Staci began to notice accounting discrepancies, followed shortly by the discovery of mountains of unpaid, overdue bills. She ended up having to file bankruptcy. Everything pointed to embezzlement. Staci couldn't—wouldn't—believe it.

She'd come to John to have a final word with Janie and learn the truth.

When sufficient time had passed, John began to rouse himself from his feigned trance. "I have placed the message," he said solemnly.

Staci stared back with wide eyes and wet her lips. "Wh-When will I know?"

"By tomorrow I should have an answer. Let's make another appointment for three o'clock." John withdrew his hands from hers.

"What if it's true?" Staci asked.

John knew Staci would feel betrayed if her suspicions turned out to be correct. It was that fear of betrayal that had prevented Staci from accepting the veracity of the evidence and had led her to John. "Staci, regardless of what I find out, you have to prepare yourself to move on with your life. Whether Janie stole from the business or not, you need to decide what you're going to do now."

"I know you're right. It's just so *hard*. Janie was my best friend before we became business partners. I can't believe she would lie to me and cheat me. What kind of person would do such a thing?"

"Maybe she was desperate. That's no excuse, of

course, but there's an excellent chance it wasn't personal," John said.

"Any time someone deliberately lies to you, it's personal," Staci said emphatically, getting to her feet.

John rounded the table and followed as Staci headed for the waiting room. "Remember, three o'clock tomorrow—" He stepped into the waiting room and froze in his tracks. Blood drained from his face and his skin seemed to shrink and tighten over his cheekbones.

"Tomorrow. Thank you," Staci said, walking out the door. Wrapped up in her own concerns, she barely glanced at the woman who stood in the waiting room, outside the convergence chamber door. If she had paid more attention, she would have noticed the fighter's stance and the hot fury shooting from the woman's eyes.

"Karyn." John forgot all about Staci, didn't even notice as his client departed.

"You son of a bitch." Karyn enunciated every syllable with icy contempt. Through the roar in his ears, her voice seemed to come from a distance, as if they were at opposite ends of a tunnel.

John wet his lips. "I can explain—"

"Really? This ought to be interesting," she said sarcastically. "Go ahead. Explain. Explain why you told me you were a *communications consultant* when you turned out to be fortune-teller. *A* fortune *hunter*. Explain why you deliberately deceived me!"

Each charge sliced through him, leaving him bleeding inside. "I wanted to tell you. I tried many times to tell you . . ." he broke off. It sounded lame even to his own ears. "Karyn, I'm so sorry."

"But you didn't tell me. Instead you fed me some stupid story about near death experiences! What was that all about? Do you enjoy making fun of people?"

"I wasn't making fun of you. And I didn't lie to you about the near death experiences. That part is true."

Karyn tore her gaze away and turned to the window, but not before John caught a glimpse of tears in her eyes. For a moment she said nothing.

"Even as I climbed the stairs and walked in, I didn't expect you'd be here."

"Oh, Karyn." John briefly closed his eyes, searched for the right words. "I never meant to hurt you. It was the last thing I wanted to do."

"Any time someone deliberately lies to you, it's hurtful and personal," Karyn rephrased Staci's words.

"You saw the session," he said weakly.

"It was quite an act, although not as good as the one you've performed for me these past few months. The communications consultant businessman. Very good, John." She applauded mockingly.

Her contempt set a match to his temper. "Do you think it's easy to tell people what I do? Do you think your reaction is different from everyone else's? People either see me as a joke or a fraud.

"Yes, I lied," he admitted. "I lied to protect myself. I like you and knew you'd never go out with me if I told you the truth. If I had told you what I did when we met at the restaurant that first time, that would have been our last date and you know it."

"I still had a right to know! Our whole relationship was based on deceit. Or is that the point? Is this a scam, John? Was I going to be your next con victim?"

Her accusation struck him speechless. When he found his voice, he bit out, "You'd think that of me? You know what your problem is? You use your mother's experience as a yardstick to measure everything else. You're so narrow-minded about anything that's different from your conventional life."

"You're putting the blame on me?" Karyn pressed a hand to her chest.

"I think you share a part, yes. You didn't make it easy for me." He looked at her unflinchingly.

She turned on her heel and walked out.

* * *

Karyn stumbled to her car, scarcely able to see through her tears as darts of betrayal and loss stabbed at her from all sides. How could he have a carried on a charade and pretended to care for her for months? He knew how she felt, what had happened to her mother. He must have been laughing at her all along. What a fool she was.

Seeing him in action during that session was like undergoing surgery without anesthesia. Wracked by pain, she stumbled to her car. On autopilot, she drove over, a haze of anguish obscuring everything. How long she'd sat in her car in her driveway, she didn't know. It was only when a neighbor knocked on her window that she realized she'd found her way home.

"Are you okay?" Concern was etched into the neighbor's expression.

Karyn blinked, wiped at the tears streaming down her face. It would be useless to deny something was wrong. "I, uh, just, uh broke up with my boyfriend. I'm a little upset, but I'll be okay."

She loved him. Breaking up and walking away was like tearing off a limb. It left her with a void she didn't think would ever be filled. John's betrayal hurt far worse than being jilted by Drew.

"Are you sure? Would you like to come over for a cup of coffee?"

The neighbor was trying to be nice, but Karyn wanted to scream. "That's very kind of you," Karyn forced herself to be pleasant. "But no thank you. I, uh, have to take care of a few things."

"If you change your mind, give me a call."

Karyn faked a smile. "Thank you."

The neighbor headed back to her house, and Karyn hurried inside before she became the object of additional pity or speculation. Rigidly holding the tears at bay, she called in sick at work for the next day.

"You sound hoarse," her boss said. "I hope you don't have that flu that's going around."

"I'm not sure how long I'll be out," Karyn said, wishing her problem was influenza. She didn't know how long it would be before she felt like herself again.

"Just take care of yourself. You don't want to spread it around," her boss said.

Chapter
Twenty

"What?" John snarled. "Go away."

Bright, cheerful morning sunlight streamed in through the gaps in the blinds and darkened his already stormy mood. Stanley pawed the bed and whined, his head cocked at a quizzical angle as if to wonder he why hadn't been taken for his morning run.

Or why his master had stayed up till the early hours of the morning drinking until he staggered into bed and passed out. Or why his nightly dinner had become a fifty-pound bag of dry food sliced open and left on the basement floor.

John focused on Stanley as best he could. The crack of light hurt his head, which pounded with the rhythm of jungle tom-toms. His stomach churned, and his mouth felt like a small, furry creature had crawled inside and died.

Stanley whined beseechingly and placed a paw on the bed.

"Go away," John growled. He pulled the blanket over his head and turned his back to the dog. The edge of the bed depressed, and Stanley began pawing at the blanket, slowly pulling it off John.

John grimaced as he turned his head toward the dog whose face was only inches away. "Jeez, your breath is worse than mine." Stanley licked at John's face.

"Woof," Stanley retorted.

John glared at the dog, but Stanley stood his ground, his tongue lolling out of his mouth, dripping saliva onto the bed, making little wet patches on the blue sheets.

"All right." John groaned as he rolled out of bed, his stiff muscles forced to move. It had been two days since everything had blown up in his face. Two days, and nothing had improved.

Naked, he staggered to the window and opened the blinds, uncaring if the neighbors saw him. He flinched as light filled the room.

When his eyes adjusted, he stumbled to the bathroom to relieve himself. He paused in front of the mirror. "Christ, you're ugly," he said to his reflection. Red-rimmed, bloodshot eyes squinted over a stubbled chin. His hair stood at sharp angles like the spikes favored by punk rockers.

John sniffed his armpit and felt his eyes well up from the smell. He searched his memory but had no recent recollection of showering. He did recall canceling his appointments, buying several bottles of Scotch, and sitting outside as the rain soaked him to the skin and diluted his drink. But was that last night or the night before?

He swallowed three aspirin, then drank long and hard from the faucet. He remained under the stinging blast of the shower until the water ran cold, then got out and donned a ragged pair of gym shorts and a T-shirt splattered with old oil stains. He shoved sockless feet into a pair of tennis shoes, then ushered Stanley into the Explorer.

Today's run would not be taken his own neighborhood.

* * *

The sky was painted a dismal gray over a wildly crashing surf, but the beach was deserted. John alighted from the truck and lowered the tailgate so Stanley could scramble out. He pulled at the leash as John ambled to the shore. "Slow, Stanley. Slow."

Slow didn't exist in Stanley's vocabulary.

John relented and disconnected the leash from his collar. Stanley zigzagged across the sand, barking excitedly, charging good-naturedly at a sea gull which took wing out of reach.

John ignored the dog's antics, his thoughts drifting like flotsam bobbing direction-less in the ocean. Dozens of times since the breakup he'd picked up the phone to call Karyn but had hung up before he finished dialing. What could he say? Even if by some miracle she forgave him for lying, the more significant matter of his occupation still existed.

Nothing could change what he was.

For the millionth time, he wondered where she was, what she was doing, if she was feeling anything close to what he was feeling. His gut twisted into a knot. Food was unpalatable, but alcohol went down easy enough— he'd downed enough shots in the past couple of days to know that.

He rubbed his eyes with the back of his hand. Stanley was darting back and forth, his nose nudging something in the sand. A crab, John saw as he neared. He left the dog with his discovery and walked on. Stanley would find him when he was ready. The tide washed over his sneakers filling them with water and sand. Making squishing noises, he walked until he came to a promontory of rocks jutting out into the ocean.

He stepped gingerly over the sharp edges. When he got to the other side, his gaze zeroed in on a lone figure on the beach digging for clams, her unrestrained blond hair blowing in the breeze. His heart contracted.

Karyn.

A wash of emotion—joy, anger, fear—surged through him. His heart began to pound madly and his knees weakened to the point of collapse.

She looked up as he neared.

It wasn't her.

The woman was shorter, stockier than Karyn and had an unremarkable face. "Morning," she said in a voice that could never be mistaken for Karyn's.

"Morning," John mumbled, avoiding her eyes and picking up his pace. He felt foolish. It was going to be a rough ride if he was shaken by every blonde he saw.

His knees buckled as Stanley plowed into him from behind, a piece of driftwood in his mouth and hope in his eyes. John took the stick and apathetically tossed it a few feet away. Stanley caught it before it touched the ground and brought it back. Hoping to deter the dog, John flung it into the ocean.

Stanley charged into the foaming surf and returned to drop the stick at John's feet, then shook himself, sending water flying through the air, splattering John with its spray.

Stanley's tail swayed vigorously and John could have sworn the dog was grinning at him.

"You," John poked his index finger at the dog, "know better than that."

"Woof!" Stanley wiggled.

John laughed, a rusty sound, and dropped to his haunches to bury his face in the dog's neck, which smelled vaguely like a wet wool blanket. When he released him, a large wet patch covered the front of his T-shirt.

"Go get it!" John flung the stick as hard as he could. Stanley raced after it with a loping stride. As John played with Stanley on the beach, he was almost able to forget.

* * *

On the drive home, the clouds opened to drop buckets of rain on Seattle, tapering off to a misty drizzle by the time John pulled into his driveway. Two little figures and one larger one hunched in raincoats were making a beeline for his doorstep.

John got out the truck. "Sandy?" He recognized his sister despite the hood pulled over her face. "What are you doing here?"

"You forgot, didn't you?" his sister accused.

"Forgot?" John racked his brain.

"Reid and I are going away this weekend. You volunteered to baby-sit."

Actually, she'd drafted him, but the result was the same. John swore silently. "Sorry. I took Stanley for a run and time got away from me."

Sandy glanced around pointedly, and John realized Stanley was still in the Explorer, his nose pressed against the window. When John lowered the tailgate so Stanley could scramble out, he noticed the car parked at the curb.

Reid lifted his hand in a small wave. John turned his head, thoughts of Caitlin and the Jacuzzi scene flashing through his mind.

"Here kids, take Stanley inside." John opened the front door. They ran in, tearing off their raincoats, dropping them on the floor.

"Do you want to come in for a moment?" John stood on the doorstep.

Sandy glanced at the car where Reid drummed his fingers on the steering wheel. "No, we gotta run. Chelsea had a slight fever last night, but she seems okay now. Watch her closely, though."

Sandy rummaged through her purse and pressed a folded sheet of paper into John's hand. "Here's the address and phone number of the inn, the pediatrician's name, the emergency numbers."

"Everything will be okay," John assured her.

"Justin's going through a phase. He won't eat anything green."

"Me neither," John said. "If there's anything—" The blast of a horn drowned his words. Reid motioned for Sandy.

"Gotta go." She peered inside the open door. Chelsea and Justin were sprawled on top of Stanley on the floor watching TV. "Kids, say good-bye to Mom!"

"Bye, Mom," they said without looking up.

"Come here!"

Glancing at each other in resignation, they trooped over. Sandy hugged and kissed Chelsea who wound her arms around her mother's neck. "Bye Mommie," she said. "Bye Daddeee!" she yelled in a piercing voice. Reid waved back.

Sandy planted a kiss on Justin's forehead. He squirmed in her embrace.

"Be good. Both of you," she commanded, and ushered them both inside.

Reid gave a little toot of the horn. John resisted the urge to flip him the one finger salute. Instead, he said to Sandy, "Have a good time and don't worry about the kids."

"I won't. I'm looking at this weekend as the beginning of something new."

* * *

"I'm hungry," Justin said. John had no sooner shut the door than his niece and nephew swarmed over him.

"Uncle John, read me a story!" Chelsea called.

"I'm really hungry," Justin continued.

"I want a story. Read me a story, Uncle John."

"I don't know any stories," John answered. His headache was starting up again.

"Can't you make them up? Daddy makes up stories all the time," Chelsea said, her tone revealing John had fallen short in her estimation.

"Let's have lunch first, and then I'll see what I can do in the story department."

John headed for the kitchen with the children trailing behind him. He opened the refrigerator and peered into its barren interior. "How about some baking soda?" he asked.

"Noooo." Chelsea shook her head violently. "I don't like baking soda."

"Pizza?"

"Yeah!" Justin yelled.

"Pizza, pizza." Chelsea sang.

John shepherded the kids into the truck and drove them to a pizza parlor. Justin had argued for the kiddie pizza place, where they had games, life-size puppets walking around, and blaring music. John knew he wouldn't be able to stand the commotion, so he overruled Justin and took them to an adult restaurant.

Chelsea spilled her Coke twice and Justin once before John learned to fill their glasses only half full. Justin went through all the change in John's pocket on the single video game machine in the small alcove of the pizza parlor. John watched as Chelsea downed once piece after another. When she started to reach for her fourth, John stopped her.

"I think you've had enough," he said.

"Noooo."

"Yes," he said.

"No." She reached for another piece.

John pulled the plate out of her reach. "Chelsea, you've already had lunch. If you eat more than this, you'll be sick."

"Yeah, you'll puke all over. It will be green and ugly." Justin made retching noises.

"I won't."

She did. Halfway home, he watched in the rear view mirror as Chelsea upchucked all down the front of her shirt and onto the interior of the Explorer. John pressed the accelerator and racing home, Chelsea wailing like a siren. Justin laughed, snorting through his nose, which made Chelsea cry harder.

Justin tumbled out of the truck, barely waiting for it to stop. He made choking noises. "It stinks! It stinks." He jumped up and down.

He wasn't kidding. The interior of the truck reeked with a sour stench. John jumped out the driver's and took a deep breath before going around to the back where Chelsea was buckled in. Her face was red from crying, and she'd made a mess of her shirt, the seat, and the floor of the Explorer.

"Shit!" John swore under his breath. He stared at his niece and he knew with absolute certainty that he didn't want to touch her. John gingerly unsnapped Chelsea's seat belt. "Okay." He stepped back. "Let's go. Out of the truck."

Chelsea peered at the ground. "I can't. It's too high."

"Oh, Chelsea." John sighed. He lifted her out of truck. Chelsea reached to wrap her arms around his neck.

"No," he said. "Don't touch Uncle John." He set her down.

As quickly as they had started, her tears stopped, staining little rivulets on her face. Her eyelashes were wet spikes. "I'm dirty," she said.

"I think this calls for a bath," John agreed.

* * *

John installed the kids in front of the electronic babysitter to watch one of their favorite cartoons and went to clean the mess in the Explorer. Hunched in the back seat with a bucket of soap and water, he heard the clatter and clank of an old engine. He peered over the back-seat and spied a large clunker with rusted, dented fenders creeping along the street. As it passed his house, it accelerated, zooming down the road in a cloud of smelly exhaust. Out of the corner of his eye, he caught a glimpse of the driver. His heart and stomach took off in opposite directions but he stood rooted to the spot, unable to look away until the car disappeared.

Karyn.

No, he corrected himself. It was probably just another blonde he'd mistaken for her like the woman at the beach. Karyn drove a red Miata, not a clunker held together by rust.

Suddenly, the mess in the Explorer didn't matter anymore. "My life stinks. My truck stinks. Perfect." John tossed the rag in the bucket and returned to the house.

* * *

Stupid. Stupid. Stupid. Karyn berated herself. She pressed the gas pedal closer to the floor and resisted the urge to duck as she sped by John's house. What's the matter with you, acting like a teenager? He probably saw you!

One minute she was home in her robe watching insipid daytime soaps, eating everything chocolate she could find, and the next moment she'd surrendered to the urge to cruise by his house.

Seeing him outside triggered the pain she had tried so hard to anesthetize. The breakup didn't trouble him, as evidenced by his ability to perform mundane tasks like washing the car.

Maybe he didn't recognize her. She was driving another car, borrowed from a coworker since her Miata was in the garage. Getting the car serviced was the first back-to-normal thing she had been able to force herself to do. The rest of the time she found herself elbows-deep in a post-mortem autopsy of the failed relationship.

She had to get over him, get on with her life. And, at the least, go back to work. Tomorrow she'd give it a try, but first she had to do something she'd been putting off.

* * *

The phone rang a half a dozen times before it was picked up.

"Hello?"

"It's me," Karyn said. "Can you talk for a minute?"

"Thank God you called." Relief echoed in Celine's voice. "I've been so worried about you."

"I know. I should have returned your messages

sooner. I've been out-of-sorts and wasn't ready to face the world."

"I'm so sorry for what happened, for being the one to tell you."

"I'm glad you did. It was a shock but God only knows how long it would have been before I found out. It was just like you said."

"You went to his office then?"

"I saw him in session. I can't believe people fall for that stuff. He did everything but saw a woman in half and pull a rabbit out of a hat."

"There's a lot of vulnerable, gullible people out there."

Karyn gave a self-deprecating snort. "I'm one of them. I should have let you run him through the computer."

"He lied to you, Karyn. There was no way you could have known. Don't blame yourself. What you need to do now is focus on healing. Do something good for yourself. Treat yourself to a day at the spa. Get out of the house. There's an art show at the museum that I hear is pretty good."

"I don't think I'm ready for that." Karyn's mouth twisted wryly. "I have the tendency to burst into tears for no good reason. Little things, memories, set me off. He was right about one thing. If only he'd told me the truth in the beginning, I never would have had anything to do with him."

"And you shouldn't have. He's a charlatan and a con man."

Karyn hesitated. "But are you sure? You said yourself you didn't have any hard evidence," she argued.

"Karyn, you're rationalizing. You're feeling bad

over the breakup and you're trying to find an excuse to go back to him."

"I just have a hard time matching the John I know with the guy you say he is."

"Karyn, you saw it with your own eyes."

Suki jumped up on Karyn's lap, settling in. Karyn stroked the cat, who closed her eyes and began to purr. Life was simple as a warm lap and a soft hand when you were a cat, Karyn mused.

"You haven't discovered anything new about him, have you?" Karyn found herself asking.

"Officially or unofficially?"

"Either."

"Nothing. As I told you, the investigation is officially over."

"Well, you see . . . " Karyn clutched at the straws.

"All that means, Karyn, is that the guy is smooth as polished stone. But one of these days, he'll crack. He'll slip up and I'll nail his ass."

Chapter
Twenty-one

John was in the basement, building shelves, driving nails into the wood, the metal hammer sparking off the steel head of the nails.

One nail. Two nails. Thwap. Thwap. Thwap.

He hammered a dozen flat-heads into the two-by-four and then stepped back to admire his handiwork.

Thwap. Thwap. The pounding continued, the clash of metal against metal ringing in his ears, even though he'd stopped working. Confused, he stared at the shelves as the sound grew louder.

With a jolt, he awakened. He blinked and glanced at the clock on the bedside table.

Thwap. Thwap.

John realized someone was banging on the door, leaning against the door buzzer.

He jumped out of bed, grabbing a robe and a baseball bat as he hurried downstairs, switching on lights as he went.

Halfway down he heard a voice calling his name.

"John! John! Open up."

"Sandy?" John turned on the porch light. "What's going on?" He opened the door. "Why are you here? It's the middle of the night!"

Wild, puffy, bloodshot eyes met his, before she pushed past him. "Where's Justin and Chelsea?" She started to dart up the stairs.

John grabbed her arm, turning her to face him. She flailed against him, but he held on. "Tell me what's wrong."

"John, stop!" Her voice rose, then fell. "Just let me go," she spoke slowly, deliberately, a warning that her carefully imposed self-control could snap like an old rubber band. She pushed against his chest, holding him off. "I have to get the kids and leave."

He stared at her. "I don't understand. *What* is going on? What about your weekend? What happened that you couldn't wait until morning to get the kids?"

"The weekend is off," she said in a monotone. "Please let me go. You're right. There's no need to wake Justin and Chelsea. I'll get them in the morning."

She sounded reasonable, but John was still reluctant to release her.

"Really," she assured him.

John let go of her arms.

Frenetic energy spent, Sandy shuffled to the door. "I'll be back first thing in the morning."

"Sandy, please tell me what's wrong."

Her back to him, she said, "Reid wants a divorce" and burst into tears.

"Oh, my God, Sandy." John gently turned her around and hugged her. "I'm so sorry."

"I thought th-this was going to be a ro-ro-romantic weekend and instead he told me he wanted a divorce."

Her tears soaked his robe. "Come on." Reaching around her, John slammed the door shut. "Let's go into the other room." He led his sister into the living room, steered her to the sofa.

Reid was an asshole, no doubt about it. There also was no doubt that, in the long run, his sister would be better off without him. But this was no time to tell her those things.

Sandy choked. "I know we've been having problems, but I never thought it would come to this."

"Did he say why?" John asked.

Sandy pulled back. Her eyes were red, swollen slits. She fumbled in her purse for a Kleenex and then blew her nose loudly. "I've been having an affair. Reid found out."

"What?!" John's jaw dropped.

She nodded. "Pretty terrible, huh?"

"But what about Caitlin?" The outburst tumbled out.

"I think Reid started to see her out of revenge because I was seeing Griffith. He's one of the associates at the law firm."

"You knew about Caitlin?"

Sandy nodded. "I think when he brought her to the house, that was the wake-up call. I'd already stopped seeing Griffith, and I realized we were in serious trouble. I knew then that I'd made a terrible mistake and I wanted to save my marriage. I hoped that this weekend would be the first step."

"R-R-Reid was working long hours. We both were. But he seemed to lose interest in our marriage—in me. Griffith made me feel special. Everybody needs to feel special." She started to cry, her shoulders shaking with her sobs. "I've screwed everything up."

John stroked her hair, but was at a loss for words. He'd cast Reid as the villain, but Sandy had played a major role in the disintegration of their marriage as well.

"H-he-he says," Sandy hiccoughed, "he can't trust me." Her tear-filled eyes met his. "What am I going to do?"

John raked his hands through his hair. The whole thing had taken on a surreal quality. Any minute now the clock would ring, or Justin would come bounce on the bed and wake him up, and everything would be normal again.

Sandy had always been the good one.

If she'd seemed a little lost lately, a little less sure of herself, she'd at least done what was expected. She never did anything weird like commune with spirits. She worked in a respectable profession, had married well, and had presented their parents with two grandchildren.

But it hadn't stopped her from ruining her relationship.

"Where's Reid now?" John asked gently.

She shrugged and said in a small voice, "I don't know. We got to the bed and breakfast. We were there, maybe an hour, and Reid told me it just wasn't going to work. He couldn't stop thinking about me and Griffith. He said he hated me. Not for the affair, but for what I made him do.

"Do you know what if feels like to have your husband tell you he hates you? Those were the last words he spoke to me. On the drive home, he never said a word. We got to the house and he packed his bags and left."

John rocked her as she cried until her tears subsided into hiccoughs. "Stay here tonight. I'll get you a pillow and some sheets."

* * *

On leaden feet, John trudged down the stairs in the morning to find his sister sleeping prone on the sofa, her arms clutching the pillow, while Justin and Chelsea sat cross-legged on the floor watching a soundless cartoon.

"Ssh," Chelsea cautioned. "Mommie's sleeping."

"I see that," he whispered back. "Why don't you two watch the TV in my bedroom, then you can turn on the sound?"

"'kay," Justin agreed, and the two scrambled to their feet and ran upstairs. John switched off the TV and padded to the kitchen to make coffee.

He drank the first cup standing at the counter. His headache of the day before had disappeared—surprising since it had taken a long time before he fell asleep after Sandy had arrived. He was working on his third cup when she appeared, clothes rumpled and creased, hair tangled, eyes swollen to slits.

"Hi," she croaked.

"Hi." He didn't ask how she felt. He could tell by looking at her. "Coffee?"

"Please." She sank down at the table.

John handed her a mug of the black brew, which she gulped immediately, then grimaced. "This is awful!" she choked.

John grinned. "Just like Mom used to make."

"I'm sorry about last night." Sandy examined the liquid in her cup.

"It's all right. You're family. I've seen you do worse," John joked.

A trace of a smile crossed her lips. "Where are the kids?"

"Upstairs watching TV."

"Did they give you any trouble?"

John thought of the umpteen glasses of spilled soda and milk, Justin teasing his sister incessantly, the constant barrage of questions, Chelsea puking in the truck. "No," he denied.

"Liar," Sandy accused. "I know my kids."

"They were perfect angels. Just like you and I were."

"Now I know you're lying." Sandy took a sip of her coffee, then stared into the black depths of the cup. John knew she was thinking about Reid.

"At least things are working for you," she said, after a long stretch of silence. "For you and Karyn."

John sighed. "That's another story for another day."

She caught the edge in his voice. "Oh, no! What happened?"

"We broke up. She found out I worked as a spiritual advisor before I could tell her."

"*You never told her?*"

"I could never find the right words or the right time."

Sandy gave a short, mirthless laugh. "We really are twins, aren't we?"

John covered his sister's hand. "Things will work out for the best, as they're supposed to."

"Is that the way *you* feel?"

He thought for a moment, hesitated before answering. "I'm in a different situation." He shook his head. He would have said more, but his niece and nephew came running into the kitchen.

"Chelsea threw up in Uncle John's car!" Justin yelled as his sister flung herself into Sandy's arms.

John's eyes met Sandy's. Any further discussion of their problems had to be postponed.

* * *

The door slammed and silence descended like the thick fog that sometimes grounded planes at SeaTac airport. The relief he'd expected to find with the solitude didn't materialize; instead, troubled emotions rushed in to fill the void.

Guilt. Remorse. He couldn't help but see the parallels between his relationship with Karyn and his sister's marriage. They'd each handled their problems in the same way, by thinking that deception could somehow have a positive end. He'd had something good, and he'd blown it by not being honest and up-front.

John raked his hands through his hair, then massaged his tired eyes. It didn't seem fair that you only got one chance with the important things in life. One strike and you're out. His mind played the mantra of the broken-hearted: If he could do it over again, he'd do things differently.

* * *

Karyn was nursing a cup of chamomile tea when the phone rang. Listlessly, she reached for it. It was probably her mother, or Celine campaigning to get her out of the house.

She picked up the receiver. "Hello?"

There was no forthcoming response.

"Hello?" she repeated.

"Did I wake you?" John's voice floated through the receiver.

As if suddenly stricken by Parkinson's disease, Karyn's hand began to shake, her cup rattling against the saucer. Quickly, she put it down before she poured the hot tea in her lap. She felt like a car driven by a beginning driver who kept one foot on the brake and one on the gas—racing, but going nowhere.

"What do you want?" She struggled to keep her tone normal.

"Just to talk." He sounded hesitant, unsure. She rejoiced at his discomfort, a vengeful thrill that played tug-of-war with a deep longing to see him.

"So talk." Her voice rang cold, even to her own ears. No matter how much she ached to be with him, to talk to him, she wouldn't give in. She couldn't.

"I know I did everything wrong, but I can't just leave things the way they are."

She said nothing, but squeezed her eyes shut in a futile attempt to stop from crying.

"Are you okay?" The concern in his voice sliced through her.

A flare of anger enabled her to speak. "Use your psychic power and figure it out!"

"Karyn, I'm so sorry." John sounded miserable. "I liked you so much, and after what you said about your mother, I was afraid you wouldn't want to see me. I wish I could set the clock back and meet you for the first time again."

"You mean that's not one of your special powers?" Her fingers closed around the delicate teacup. She could picture herself crushing it into shards of glass. "Do you take VISA?"

"Do I take VISA?" John repeated her words. "What are you talking about?"

"Do you take VISA cards? My mother's fortune-teller took VISA, Master Card and American Express. My mother's still paying off the bills."

"This isn't about your mother, Karyn." An undercurrent of anger slipped beneath his words.

"It's about you being a psychic and lying to me about it. Oh, I forgot. You're a communications expert. Tell me, do you give spirits tips on how to present themselves during media interviews? Or maybe you're Elvis Presley's new publicist."

"Stop it!" John bit out. "Yes, I lied and I can't undo that. But the fact is, you don't know as much about me as you think you do. You're judging me based on what happened to your mother. I didn't cheat your mother! Do you hear me? I had nothing to do with what happened to your mother! And if you weren't so boxed in by your narrow little world, you might just see that."

"If you're so honest, why are you being investigated by the police?"

"Was investigated. Past tense. It's over. And do you know why? Because they didn't find anything." He paused, but before Karyn could respond, he said, "Why can't you give me the benefit of the doubt?" His voice seemed to sag underneath the weight of weariness.

"I believe what I see. And I saw it all in your office the other day."

"You didn't see it all."

"I saw all I needed to see." She couldn't maintain a serious relationship with a man who did things on a day-to-day basis that she thought were dishonest. A chasm separated their belief systems, their values. Even if she overlooked this, it still would never work between her and John.

"I'm sorry." Her simple words carried a lot of meaning.

"I guess that's it," he said.

Without a good-bye, Karyn hung up the phone. She yanked the cord out of the wall and went into the kitchen to unplug the extension in there. She was sobbing by the time she reached the phone.

* * *

At the click, John grabbed the phone and threw it against the wall. The cord snapped, the phone shattered and the impact dented the plaster.

"That's all, folks," he said aloud.

He felt something wet on his face, and he realized he was crying.

"Damn her," he swore.

He tried to envision life without her, but could only see a string of broken relationships. What other end could there be? If the woman he loved couldn't accept what he did, how could anybody else?

He needed to get away, take time to regroup, recover. Maybe close the business for a while and take a real vacation. A trip along the coast, maybe Vancouver, or—

The spark of interest died as he realized those were the kinds of trips he would have liked to have taken with Karyn. He looked around his living room, noting the overstuffed sofa, the large brick fireplace, the piles of newspapers and Stanley sprawled on the floor. This was all he had to show for thirty-six years of living.

He flopped onto the sofa and stared out the window.

When he roused himself, hours later, he'd made a decision.

Twenty-two

Chapter

The mist swirled around him, filling him, if not with calm, then with the sense of purpose and perspective that the Other Side always brought to him. But as he reveled in the soothing effect, he realized he couldn't solve his problems from the Other Side. That had to be done with his feet planted firmly on the ground.

"I won't be back for a while. I need to sort out my life," John spoke into the mist and to his grandmother. His grandmother's support was important to him. It was because of her that he'd begun coming to the Other Side. He didn't want to disappoint her.

"I understand," she said.

"It's something I have to do. I feel like I haven't been living the life I was given."

"I understand," his grandmother repeated.

"I *have* to come here. It's a part of me. To not come here would be like asking a fish to give up water, a bird to give up flying. But I need to make some changes. There has to be compromise, so that my life here can co-exist with my physical existence."

"I understand."

"It'll be a while—I don't know how long—before I come back. I will come back, though," John promised.

"Of course."

"I hope you can understand."

His grandmother gave a little laugh. "John, have

you been listening to me? I said I understand. We all come to a point in our lives where we have to stop to evaluate ourselves and our lives to ensure we haven't detoured, that we still want to go where we're headed. I've been expecting this from you."

"I feel so aimless, so disconnected. Like someone pulled the rug out from under me."

"And when you picked yourself up and looked around, everything had changed. The world wasn't the same place, and you weren't the same person."

"I feel like two people. One who comes here; one who wants to be with Karyn. I'm being pulled in separate directions. I need to find out which one I really am."

"Questioning nurtures the soul," she said with approval. "Following life's path is like sailing. You can't always go in a straight line and you have to adjust your course to stay on track. By taking the time to examine your life, you're reassessing your path and making sure that it's really where you want to go.

"I had my share of ups and downs when I was alive," she recalled. "Did I tell you the time your grandfather lost his job during the Great Depression? He was laid off at the meat packing plant and didn't tell me. Every day, he got up, got dressed and left, like he was going to work."

"How did you find out?" John asked. He hadn't heard the story.

"The bank foreclosed on the house. It was the most difficult time of my life, but in the end, it made us both stronger and we took care to not repeat the past mistakes. You'll find that the things you think are permanent, aren't, and the things you think aren't, are."

"Karyn dumped me," John said. "That's pretty permanent. She never wants to see me again."

"I know," his grandmother said.

John allowed himself to float, a raft in a sea of nothingness, absorbing the energy of the Other Side without sending or receiving communication signals. It was peaceful, soothing, a balm to the turmoil that gnawed at him.

"You have been granted a privilege—a very rare privilege," his grandmother broke into the void. "But keep in mind you are only a visitor here. You've been granted a visa, not citizenship."

He sensed a warning in her words, but because it was too much trouble to glean the meaning, he allowed her thoughts to bounce off his consciousness, flat stones skipping across a tranquil pond.

"Maybe I'll get a real job," he said.

"What you do isn't real?"

"I don't want to live on the fringe anymore. I'm an outcast. If I ever meet someone like Karyn again, I don't want my occupation to come between us."

John laughed mockingly. "Maybe I'll go into communications after all."

* * *

Life seeped back into his limbs, leaving a tingling in its wake. Pins and needles rippled through his body. He waited for the sensation to pass before he rose from the sofa to continue packing up his office.

He felt better about his decision after talking to his grandmother. Going to the Other Side usually filled him with peace and he saw the world with greater clarity. Clarifying his own life however, required that he do it as his corporeal self. He was like a mermaid: To experience life on land, he would have to give up his tail.

Unlike a mortal mermaid, he *would* return to the sea, to the Other Side. He had to. From beyond, the Other Side called to him, tugged at his soul. He couldn't—didn't want—to resist it forever.

But for now, he'd postpone his travels. He'd already notified his clients. They expressed disappointment, of course, but surprisingly, they supported his decision. In some strange way, that made him feel even guiltier. They had to surrender their only link to their departed loved ones while John struggled to find himself.

Life offered a multitude of opportunities, and he was determined to pursue some of them. He'd prefer to have Karyn by his side, but if that wasn't meant to be, then eventually, one day, he'd find someone else.

John folded a flat cardboard carton into a box. Beginning with the file cabinet, he began to empty drawers. He had had a lot of clients over the years. Hundreds probably. Some came once and that was enough. Some came several times. Some, like the late Mrs. Boswell, had come for years.

He'd miss them. He had gotten to know them, had become a part of their lives. He had been invited to weddings, christenings, birthday parties, bar mitzvahs.

John wondered what his next move would be. He could write a book. *I Was a Messenger to the Dead* by John—no, Jonathan Metcalf. It had a ring to it. He laughed to himself.

Maybe he should go back to school. Get an advanced degree. Maybe an MBA.

The bell on the front door rang, touching off a stab of anxiety. He recalled the last time he'd been surprised by a visitor. Hesitantly, John peered into the waiting room.

"You!" he sputtered.

"Packing up, I see?" Celine Dufresne eyed the boxes and furniture pushed to one wall.

"What do you want?" He could not forget the role Celine had played in the mess that had become his life.

"I've come to pay my respects," she answered. Her choice of words was appropriate; a part of him had died.

"Pay your respects or collect your winnings?"

"Is there a difference?" she shot back.

"In your case, no," he said coldly.

They both started as the door opened.

"I hope I'm not interrupting." Mrs. Pembroke, one of John's long-time clients, appeared. She was at least ninety, and walked hunched over in such a way that made her appear smaller than she actually was.

"Mrs. Pembroke, you're always welcome." John took her knobby, veined hand in his.

Mrs. Pembroke beamed a perfect dentured smile, and handed John a folded Afghan, crocheted in rainbow colors.

"I'm so sorry you're leaving," she said. "I took an extra painkiller for my arthritis so I could finish this and settle my bill before you left."

"There was no need for you to rush, Mrs. Pembroke. But thank you. It's beautiful," John said.

Celine's looked as if she had swallowed something bitter. "You knitted this?" she asked Mrs. Pembroke.

"Crocheted, dear, crocheted," Mrs. Pembroke corrected.

"As payment for his services?"

"I told Mr. Metcalf I made afghans for all my grandchildren and my great grandchildren, too. When my social security check got delayed, he suggested I could give him one of my afghans as payment." Mrs. Pembroke lowered her voice and said in a conspiratorial tone, "He's not married, you know, and doesn't have wife to make things like that for him."

Under Celine's watchful eye, John chatted with Mrs. Pembroke, until the elderly lady wished him well and bid her good-bye. "My grandson is waiting in the car for me. He's a good boy, but he gets a bit impatient sometime. I wish he could be more like Mr. Metcalf."

"Your clients pay you in afghans?" Celine said after Mrs. Pembroke departed.

"I also accept cash and casseroles," John said.

"Sounds like your investigation was incomplete."

"How do you stay in business?"

John glanced pointedly at the stacked boxes.

To his surprise, she flushed.

"Most of my clients are able to pay. When they can't we've made other arrangements," John said.

"I had to tell her," Celine said.

"Is that an apology or a boast?" He resumed packing to show her he didn't care what she did.

"We had to investigate the complaint. It's the law," she said.

John glanced at her. "I don't hold it against you that you did your job. What I think is reprehensible is that once you knew that I was clean, you systematically set out to destroy my life. You attacked my business, my livelihood and ruined my relationship with Karyn."

"Perhaps we were a little overzealous, but I didn't ruin your relationship with Karyn." She leveled an accusing gaze on him. "You did that all by yourself."

* * *

Celine had heard via the grapevine that John was packing it up and a compulsion—guilt? —forced her to go and see for herself. She'd hoped the meeting would reassure her, but instead it had raised more doubts.

Although she'd refused to admit anything to John, to confess that she'd been wrong, her conscience wouldn't let her hide the truth from herself.

The investigation had revealed his clients genuinely liked, trusted, and respected him. She'd known about the casseroles and afghans. At first she'd discounted the evidence—con men were personable, charismatic. It wasn't difficult to fool the public, let alone little old widows grieving for their husbands. Even when the evidence became irrefutable, she'd persisted.

No excuse, he should have told Karyn the truth.

But as Celine's conscience forced her to admit, hers was the greater sin.

She couldn't undo everything she'd done to his reputation, his business, his relationship, but she could confess what she'd done. And, if she were lucky, maybe she'd even have a job when this was over.

She'd have a talk with Karyn, too.

* * *

Why had Celine come by? To gloat?

Probably.

Although he had decided for reasons of his own to close the business, she probably took great pleasure in seeing him packing it up. She'd misjudged him, knew it, and didn't care. That's what disturbed him the most. But, if he were honest with himself, he had to admit that Celine hadn't ruined his relationship with Karyn.

He'd known his calling was going to be problem, and he'd known his lie would compound the difficulty. He had no one to blame but himself.

When the last box was sealed and labeled, he surveyed the office, seeing the towering stacks of cartons, the empty desk, the dust flurries that had appeared despite the weekly cleaning. It was no longer his office, but another rental space ready to be leased to someone else.

This is all that's left, he thought as he switched off the lights. Tomorrow, he'd cart the stuff to his basement and then begin the hard part—figure out what to do with the rest of his life.

The phone in the reception area rang. Reluctantly, because he didn't want to speak to anyone, he answered it. Out of habit, he said, "Spiritual advisor."

"Thank God you're there. It's Dad," said a strangled, thready voice not at all like his father's booming, confident tone.

"Dad? What's wrong?"

"There's been an accident."

Chapter Twenty-three

John jerked the steering wheel, and with tires squealing, swerved into the hospital emergency entrance parking lot. The lot was full, the few open spaces marked Ambulance Reserved, Handicapped Reserved, Doctors' Reserved. Nothing, apparently, was reserved for frantic family members. He pulled into a doctor's spot.

He cut the engine, leaped from his truck and dashed into the hospital. John scanned the ER waiting room, searching for someone in authority, only peripherally taking in a young man slouched in a chair clutching a bloodied rag to his head and a middle-aged woman rocking back and forth, moaning in pain. Two receptionist cubicles were open, but both had people in line, waiting to check in.

A sign over the desk said "Please tell the receptionist immediately if you are suffering from chest pains, shortness of breath or are bleeding profusely." Another sign, a larger one, said "Payment is due when services are rendered. Please have your insurance card ready."

When it seemed like he couldn't take the waiting anymore, he made it to the front of the line. "I'm here to see my sister, Sandy Paxton," he said before the medical receptionist could greet him.

"Your name?"

"John Metcalf."

"I'll check. I'll be right back," she said, and disappeared through the swinging door behind her cubicle.

Moments later she returned. "The doctor is with her now. Have a seat. The nurse will be with you shortly."

"How is she? What condition is she in?" he asked.

"The nurse will speak to you in a few moments," the receptionist replied.

Frustrated, John paced around the rectangle of connected plastic chairs, keeping his eye on ER door as he waited for the nurse. Like a recording on a continuous loop, the brief, shattering phone call replayed itself in his mind.

"There's been an accident. A car accident. It's Sandy. She's not doing well. Your mom and I are at the emergency room," his father had said.

"I'll be right there," John had responded and hung up without asking what hospital his sister was in, a fact which only occurred to him now.

"John?"

He looked up to see his parents. His mother's face was pinched white by worry, and she leaned against her husband as if she would collapse without support. His father's face bore the look of a shell-shocked soldier.

"How is she? What happened?" John jumped to his feet.

Steve shook his head. "It doesn't look good—"

His mother choked a garbled sound of despair.

"She was in a car accident. With Reid," Steve continued in a deadpan voice. "The car flipped over. Rolled a few times. She has head injuries. She's unconscious. The paramedics said witnesses said it looked as if they were arguing. The car drifted over to the shoulder. Reid over-corrected and . . ." his dad's voice trailed off.

"How's Reid?"

His dad hesitated, glanced at John's mom. "He didn't make it."

"He's dead?" John read the answer on his father's face. John closed his eyes. "Christ."

"He was conscious right after the accident. The paramedics said he kept calling for Sandy until he died."

A tightness in his chest clamped his heart in a vise, squeezing harder and harder. John pictured the accident. Sandy and Reid yelling, arguing. Reid distracted. He wondered if his parents knew that Sandy and Reid had been having problems, then realized it didn't matter.

Reid was dead. His sister might die, leaving two little kids. Or had his niece and nephew been in the car? "Justin and Chelsea? What about—"

"They're okay," his mother said through her tears. "They were with us. They're at a neighbor's now."

"John!"

All three turned. Karyn hurried toward them, her hands reaching out first to his mother. "I just heard. I'm so sorry." Karyn's eyes reflected sympathy and she held Nydia's gaze. "Please let me know if there's anything I can do."

"You can get a nurse out here to tell us what's going on," John snapped. The shock of his sister's injury wasn't enough to deaden the pain caused by Karyn's presence.

"I'll check on that right away." Karyn turned to leave.

"Wait." John touched her arm. "I'm sorry. It's not your fault. I'm just on edge."

"I understand," she said, and he read the sincere sympathy in her eyes.

"How did you hear about this?"

"Social Services was notified that there was a family in need, and I recognized the name," she said. "I won't be long." She disappeared down the corridor, the click of her heels tracking her movement. Five minutes later, she returned with a white-clad nurse.

The nurse made eye contact with each of them, silently addressing each of them, before looking at Nydia. "The doctors are doing everything they can. Your daughter has sustained a serious trauma to the head and she's in critical condition right now. We're moving her to the Intensive Care Unit. Once she's there, you'll be able to go up and see her. The doctor there will have more information. Do you know where ICU is?"

Nydia shook her head dumbly.

The nurse spelled out directions to the ICU that became increasingly convoluted.

"I'll show them where it is," Karyn offered, noticing their dazed and dismayed expressions.

With a nod, the nurse left.

The ICU door was locked and a posted sign informed them to use the phone on the wall to call the nurse to buzz them in. Karyn picked up the phone and waited. "It's ringing," she said told them.

"Hello?" she began to speak into the phone. "This is Karyn Walker from Social Services. The family of Sandy Paxton are here to see her. Okay. All right." Karyn hung up.

"They're getting her settled and said you can enter in about half an hour. Only two people at a time and you'll need to limit your visit to ten minutes."

Visit? John thought. What a euphemism. His sister lay in critical condition and he had come to visit.

"There's a waiting room around the corner," Karyn was saying.

Waiting room. Now that was an appropriate. All you did was wait. Wait for the nurse. Wait for the doctor.

Wait to see the patient. Wait.

His dad and mom settled into chairs in the waiting room, but John couldn't sit still. He paced. The path worn in the carpet from the seats to the window revealed others had done the same. He paused before the window and looked down at the parking lot. Late now, most of the cars had cleared out, and parking spaces were in abundance. A misty rain fell, shrouding the lot in fog through which the street lights glowed fuzzily. It reminded John of the Other Side and he stared for moment, searching for peace, but found none.

He turned to resume pacing and bumped into Karyn. "Sorry," he apologized brusquely.

She touched his elbow. "Why don't you sit down?"

"I can't." He nervously ran his hands through his hair.

"Come on." Karyn tugged him gently to a chair and pushed him into the seat. "Sit."

He complied and she sat next to him, clasping his hand in both of hers. In some strange way, while her presence opened wounds, it also comforted. His parents had each other. He had no one. Except Karyn. He refused to consider the consequences when the crisis ended and they parted again.

"I'm sure you have other people to see," he said, hoping she didn't.

"Right now you're the one I've come to see."

"So this is just a professional case for you."

"My shift ended an hour ago. I'm here because I want to be."

With her words, a warmth stole into his chest, beginning to thaw the ice that had seemed to settled there with the breakup. He studied their clasped hands, squeezed her fingers. Her hand tightened around his.

"Thank you," he said, still studying their hands.

Silence settled on the room, so quiet John could hear the distant whir of an elevator.

His mother broke the silence first. "I don't know what I'll do if Sandy dies," she whispered brokenly, her face wrinkled by grief. "To think I may never see my baby again—" She started to sob. "What will happen to Chelsea and Justin?"

His dad wrapped an arm around her, holding her as much for his sake as hers. John could tell his father was fighting back his own tears. The skin on his face seemed to sag as if he'd turned into an old man right before John's eyes.

Karyn gently disengaged her hand from his, and knelt beside his parents. "Nydia, just hold on. Let's see what the doctor says. Sandy is young. She's strong. She'll fight."

Watching the family drama unfold, John didn't see the white-coated woman approach.

"Mr. Metcalf? Mrs. Metcalf?"

Startled, the five of them looked up. John leaped up, and his parents tottered to their feet.

"I'm Doctor Rydell. We did a CT scan, which revealed that your daughter has suffered a serious head injury, as we'd suspected. She's in critical, but stable, condition right now. We won't know how she is until the swelling goes down."

John felt a twinge of anger. The information was nothing new. They had waited hours already for this?

"But is she going to be okay?" his mom asked for reassurance.

"We don't know." The doctor shook her head. "The next forty-eight hours will be critical."

"Can I see her?" his mother asked.

The doctor nodded. "But please keep your visit short and no more than two at a time."

His parents followed the doctor into ICU. John sank back into his seat, his wobbly legs unable to support him. He leaned his elbows on his knees and held his head in his hands. He felt Karyn place her hand softly on his leg.

How long he sat like that, he had no idea. It could have been minutes, but it seemed like years. The sound of the ICU door opening and closing roused him, and he looked up to his mom sobbing into a wadded Kleenex.

"Come on, Nid. Let's go to the cafeteria and get a cup of coffee," his dad said. "It's going to be a long night."

"No, I want to stay . . ."

"Steve is right, Nydia," Karyn said gently. "I know you're not going to want to leave the hospital, and you need to take care of yourself. John and I will come and get you if we hear anything."

"If anything happens . . ." his mother glanced over her shoulder, as her husband led her to the elevator.

"We'll call you right away. We'll be right here. Don't worry," Karyn said.

Karyn once again spoke into the waiting room phone, and the door to the ICU buzzed open. The desk nurse peered up from her paperwork as John and Karyn passed by. "Please keep your visit short," she said in a low tone, as if she were afraid of waking the patients. It would be a long time before some of the patients awoke from their comas; others would never awaken.

Artificial respirators forced air into the lungs of comatose patients and then exhaled for them, spreading the scent of death throughout the ICU. It was a death John had never before encountered. The death he knew was quiet, peaceful, restful, not this labored, wrenching process that tortured the body before reluctantly releasing the soul.

Dozens of open rooms outlined the perimeter of ICU. Inside them, machines beeped and flashed, monitoring the mostly elderly patients attached to tubes and wires. Their frailty and helplessness seemed to strip them naked and John averted his gaze.

They found Sandy in a corner room. Like the others, she appeared diminished by her condition and the machinery. A heart monitor tracked her pulse and heart rate, an EEG measured her brain waves, and a tube fed her oxygen. Her only ties to the world were the thin wires linking her to the life-prolonging machinery.

"Hey, kid," John whispered, his voice seeming to boom amidst the hissing machines.

Unconscious, Sandy's eyes remained shut, a crease furrowed between her brows as if she worried over some problem in her sleep.

He wanted to shake her until she awakened. Instead he touched her arm that rested outside the sheet. It felt lifeless and cool.

"It's cold in here. She's cold. Why don't they turn up the heat?" John focused on the mundane.

"I don't know. I think maybe they need it cool for the machines," Karyn answered.

"Machines? What about the people?" he demanded.

"I'm sure it's all right," Karyn said, trying to calm him.

"It's not. Nurse! Where's the nurse!" John called.

"John!" Karyn said in a loud whisper. "They know what they're doing." She grasped his arms and shook him gently, more a comfort than a rebuke. "It's okay. Talk to her," she said softly. "She might be able to hear you."

She spoke the truth.

Frequently, just before he slipped over to the Other Side, John could hear things. Like background noise; he was aware of it without being distracted by it. The Musak of the living world. If the noise were sharp enough, or a particularly significant phrase jumped out, it would jerk him back to his physical body.

Perhaps if he spoke to his sister, she would hear and fight her way back to consciousness. He stroked her hair, avoiding the bandages on her head, the bruises on her face.

"Some people will do anything for a little attention," John joked, keeping his tone light. "You got an ambulance ride and everything. Remember when I fell out of the tree and broke my arm? The tree Mom told me not to climb? I didn't get an ambulance. Dad drove me to the hospital and yelled at me the whole way. I did get a few days off school and Mom waited on me hand and foot. I guess it's your turn, now, huh?

"Everything's going to be okay, Sis. Don't worry. You're going to be up and out of here in no time. Mom and Dad are here. They went to the cafeteria to get a cup of coffee. Karyn is here. You remember Karyn. The kids are fine. They're at a neighbor's."

If she could hear, John hoped the omission of a mention of her husband would go unnoticed.

A nurse stuck her head in the doorway. "Just a few more minutes."

"Okay," Karyn answered.

"We have to go now. You know, hospital rules and all. We'll all be back to see you soon." He kissed her forehead. "I love you."

They returned to the waiting area, and John slumped into a chair by the window. He shook his head. "I can't stand—" his voice broke "—to see her like that!"

"Oh, John." Karyn put her arms around him and held him. "I'm so sorry." She wished she could tell him it would be all right, but the odds were it might not be.

She saw people in Sandy's condition all the time, but it didn't prepare her for the situation when it was someone she knew. She found she couldn't maintain her professional detachment seeing John and his family so distraught.

She'd begun to have doubts about cutting off the relationship with John when Celine had called her in the afternoon. Celine amended her earlier indictment of John, giving him, in fact, a character reference.

"He's packing it in," Celine had said.

"You mean you succeeded in running him out of business," Karyn had corrected.

"No. Not that I didn't try, but he was able to keep his business license. I think he's quitting because of you."

Still trying to harden her heart, Karyn answered, "It's a little late."

"His clients pay him in chickens," Celine announced, as if it should hold some special meaning for Karyn.

"What for? So he can eviscerate them during some voodoo ceremony?" Even as she said it, the sarcasm made Karyn feel ashamed.

"I didn't mean literal chickens. I mean he operates on the barter system for clients who don't have much money. One old lady gave him an afghan to settle his bill. Karyn, I screwed up. Look, I think he's a weird, but honest guy. What I'm trying to say is, if you're still interested in him, I think you could do worse."

"I'm not interested," Karyn denied.

But she was.

And with the notification of Sandy's announcement and John's appearance in the hospital, all residual anger and animosity dissipated like wisps of fog under an afternoon sun. While she didn't excuse his lying, she recognized the veracity of his accusations against her. She *had* been blinded by her mother's unfortunate experience. Nothing John could have said or done would have gained her acceptance if he'd told her the truth.

As John slumped with his head in his hands, she used the opportunity to study him. She remembered the sound of his laughter, warm and enveloping. The smoothness of his skin against hers. The fact that he would often call her in the middle of the day to say hi, just to hear her voice. His effort to mend his relationship with his father. His caring for his sister.

Celine was right. Regardless of what he did for living, he was a good man, and she cursed herself for not realizing it sooner. After the hurtful way she'd treated him, she had no right to expect anything from him, but she hoped she still had a chance.

Karyn touched his shoulder, seeking comfort as much as providing it. "The doctors are doing everything they can."

"I know." He looked at her. "I'm glad you came."

"I couldn't stay away."

"I missed you." His eyes connected with hers. She felt her eyes well with tears, and she blinked them away. "I missed you, too."

Nydia appeared with Steve who carried a cup of coffee. "Did anything happen? Did she wake up?"

"No. We saw her after you did. There's no change," John answered.

"I wouldn't expect to hear anything this soon," his dad reminded her.

"I'd better get a cup of coffee. We're probably going to be hear all night." John forced himself to his feet.

Karyn stood up. "I'll come with you."

* * *

Food Service had closed up, but the vending machine offered a sampling of sandwiches as well as hot coffee, chocolate, and tea. Though his stomach protested, John selected a chicken salad sandwich and coffee. Karyn bought a cup of hot chocolate, and they moved to a table in the corner.

John unwrapped the sandwich and mechanically chewed the tasteless lump. He forced half of it down before it became unbearable and he pushed it away. The coffee tasted stale, but it was hot and felt good going down.

"Reid was still alive for a while after the accident," John said, more to himself than Karyn.

"I know," she covered his hand.

"You never know, do you? You get up one morning thinking it's going to be a day like any other, and whamo. Everything changes. You should have seen my sister and Reid when they first got married. They were like a sappy love story in action. The whole goo-goo-eyed thing," he mused, then belated remembered that sappy love stories frequently ended tragically.

"Has someone told his family?" Karyn asked.

"I doubt it. I think Sandy said something about them going on vacation somewhere."

"Give me their names and I'll have them contacted."

John exhaled. "I don't feel so bad for Reid. He'gone to a better place. Well, maybe not a better place, but a different one that's just as good. I feel horrible for Justin and Chelsea who lost their father. For Sandy. *When*—" he emphasized the when, "she wakes up, it's going to be a tremendous blow. They were having troubles, but I think they loved each other, and in the end would have found their way." His eyes met Karyn's and she couldn't help but think it also described their own relationship.

It made her sick to her stomach to think of how close she'd come to losing John, not to death, but to separation. Thank God she'd come to her senses. John was right about Sandy. If—given Sandy's condition, and it was an *if* and not a *when*—she woke up, Reid's death would be devastating blow.

Karyn squeezed John's hand.

"You don't have to stay. I'll be okay," he said.

"I want to stay." Her eyes, intent, met his. He knew she was talking about more than the present moment. She was talking about their future.

"What about what I do?"

"It's going to take getting used to. But I'm going to try," Karyn said.

He lifted her hand to his lips and gently kissed her fingers. "Thank you." She was a lifeline, and the urge to hang onto her was strong. His sister's injury and her possible death was rawly painful, as if his skin were being flayed from his body, strip by strip. But with Karyn at his side, the pain was bearable.

They spoke in low tones on the way back to the ICU waiting area, unwilling to disturb the quiet of the deserted halls. Most of the doctors and technicians had left for the day, and while patients slept, only an occasional night nurse or a janitor walked the halls.

"I'm not afraid for her," John said in a muted voice. "For my sister I mean. Death is not to be feared. But life is not to be surrendered lightly. Life is a gift."

Chapter Twenty-four

With a jolt, John awakened. Sometime during the night, he'd fallen asleep in the stiff, uncomfortable hospital chair. Weak, early morning light filtered through the hospital window, revealing that dawn was breaking over the city.

Karyn was curled against him, her head resting on his shoulder, her hand clasping his arm. His dad wheezed quietly, stretched out, head thrown back, mouth open. His mom slumped sideways in her chair, murmuring in her sleep.

The halls and waiting rooms were still undisturbed, the day's emergencies still in the future.

So what had awakened him?

He gently slipped out of Karyn's grasp and eased her over to rest against the padded arm of the chair.

At first the ICU nurse refused to admit him.

"I'm sorry, sir, but visiting hours aren't for another two hours," she said.

"I understand," he replied, his hand gripping the telephone receiver as his mind raced ahead, searching for another answer if his power of persuasion failed. If he couldn't convince her to let him in, he was going to appropriate a lab coat and Doctor Metcalf would appear.

"I know it's hospital policy," he said in an apologetic voice. "I'm requesting an exception. My family and I have been here all night. Please, I just want to see my sister for a minute. I promise I'll leave right away."

"Well . . . all right," she said. "But this is an exception."

The door buzzed, granting him entry. "Thank you." He nodded to the nurse at the desk.

"One minute," she reminded him.

Sandy looked the same, but different. Pale, vulnerable, but peaceful somehow. Lines previously etched into her forehead were erased, replaced by smoothness. John studied the blips seesawing on the monitors. No change there.

No, wait.

Was it his imagination or were the lines imperceptibly flattening? He returned his gaze to his sister, studying her face, willing her to wake, open her eyes, speak. "Be strong, Sandy," he begged. "Please be strong. Fight. You can do it."

He tugged a chair to the bed, its metal feet scraping on the floor. Seated, he gathered Sandy's hand in his, careful not to disturb the IV inserted and taped into her arm.

Karyn found him sitting there, unmoving, his head bowed over his hands. "How is she?"

"I don't know. Something has changed, but I don't what it is."

"Everything looks normal on the monitors." Karyn regarded the blipping screens.

He shook his head. "But it's not."

The nurse appeared. "I'm sorry, sir. You'll have to leave now."

John smoothed back his sister's hair and kissed her forehead. "I'll see you later, Sis. Remember what I said. Fight!"

The ICU door had almost swung shut behind them, when he heard the nurse cry out, "Code blue!"

Fear clogging his throat, he rushed back into ICU to see the nurse pressing down on his sister's chest. "No!" he yelled and would have rushed to the bedside had Karyn not held him back.

More nurses appeared, seemingly out of nowhere, and converged on his sister's bedside. "Sir, you'll have to leave!" one shouted at him. One nurse cupped a respirator over his sister's face, while another continued with chest compressions. A third nurse dragged a crash cart to the bed.

A male nurse grabbed his arm and urged him toward the door. "Sir, you have to wait outside."

"It's my sister!" John protested. Claws of fear raked over him.

"We're doing everything we can for her."

"No!" John resisted.

"John." Karyn's grip on his arm was strong, insistent, as he tried to twist away. "It's hard, but you have to give them space to work. There's nothing you can do. You'll only get in the way," she said, not unkindly.

Though everything in him cried out against it, he allowed Karyn to lead him from the unit.

His parents had wakened and rushed to his side.

"What happened?" Like two lasers, his mom's eyes burned with intensity.

"Sandy . . . Sandy went into cardiac arrest," John choked.

"Oh, my God! Sandy! Omigod, Omigod . . ." his mother keened.

Pain, loss, anger, squeezed the breath from John's lungs. "Something was wrong!" he gasped, on the verge of hyperventilation. "*Goddamnit*, I knew something was wrong. I looked at those monitors and they looked different! Why didn't I say something! Why didn't I do something!"

"John, don't beat yourself up. It's not your fault," Karyn said. "The screens looked normal. Sandy's condition appeared the same."

"I should have done— "

"Son, she's right," Steve cut in. "All you can do is be there for her. It's in the doctor's hands. And God's."

John's eye's flashed with desperation. "I'd snatch her out of God's hands if I could."

He froze.

He *could*.

He seized Karyn by the arms. "Where can I go? Quick! I need someplace quiet. A lounge. Or a bed somewhere. Now!"

She stared as if he'd suddenly sprouted another head. "What are you talking about? Are you feeling faint? Here, sit here." She tried to propel him toward the seats. "Put your head between your legs."

"Don't you understand? There's no time!" He shook her slightly. "I have to be alone. Where can I go?"

Bewildered, she said, "There's a doctor's lounge down the hall—"

"Where?" He released her and ran into the corridor. "Which way?

"That way." She pointed. "But you can't use—"

John tore down the passageway before she could finish. Karyn ran after him. "John, wait!"

Karyn caught up with him as he barreled into the room marked "Physician's Lounge." The room was unoccupied, dark. Karyn turned on the light.

"How long?" he asked and flipped off the light switch, returning the room to darkness. Thin ribbons of light seeping through the slats of the window blinds were no match for the blackness of the room. "How long will they keep up the CPR?" John stretched out on a couch against the wall.

"I don't know . . . She's young and was in good health before the accident. They might keep it up for thirty minutes."

Karyn's gaze followed his to the clock on the wall. Ten minutes had elapsed since they had left ICU.

"She has twenty minutes left. I have five," he said.

"What are you talking about?"

"I'm bringing her back. You wanted proof near death experiences exist, this is it."

Karyn gaped at him.

John jumped up. He kissed her hard and quick on the mouth. "I love you. Whatever happens, I love you. Please, lock the door. Don't let anyone in."

He returned to the couch, conscious of his sister's life slipping away with each tick of the clock. With each passing second, the chances of reaching her grew slimmer.

Her eyes adjusting to the darkness, Karyn stumbled on stiff legs to a chair. She could hear John breathing rhythmically, inhaling deeply, and exhaling in a protracted whoosh. Her heart thumped madly, partly as a result of the circumstance, partly out some unknown, unnamed fear. Just what was she afraid of?

The answer came to her with a razor sharpness. Up to this point, she'd discounted near death experiences. But what if they were real? What if John could really do it? And if he could, what if something went wrong? Like childhood monsters, her fears loomed large and real in the darkened room.

How long she sat there, she didn't know. Time seemed to pass very slowly, but it couldn't have been more than a couple of minutes, could it? Through the dimness of the room, she could make out John's still form on the sofa. In darkness, her was sight diminished, but her hearing enhanced. The tiny lounge refrigerator emitted an annoying whine, filing away at sensitive nerve endings. The clock ticked in a regular pattern, like the internal metronome of a beating heart. Was it her imagination or did she hear John's heart beating in cadence?

Imagination.

But his respiration, she *could* detect.

Inhale. Exhale.

In. Out.

In . . .Out. . .

His breathing slowed.

In . . . . . . Out. . . . .

She held her own breath as she waited for the next inhalation. It's just his trance, she told herself, as the next breath failed to come. *It's just the refrigerator. And the clock. They're so loud, I can't hear anything.*

Except her own heartbeat.

John was still breathing, wasn't he?

She opened her mouth to call his name, then stopped. He'd told her to be quiet, and besides, none of this was real anyway. He'd simply induced a trance. It made him feel better to think he could do something. Later they could talk about this. Work it out. Now wasn't the time.

But she needed to know. To reassure herself.

She felt her way to his side, avoiding furniture and trash baskets.

She touched his chest.

It was still.

Palm flat, she pressed harder.

Karyn dipped her head and placed her ear next to his nose and mouth, praying for that little puff of breath that signaled life.

Nothing.

She'd allowed the charade to go on long enough.

"John!" She shook him. "Wake up!" she shook his shoulder.

Fear clogged her throat.

There was no response.

"Oh, my God!" Karyn ran for the lights and slammed into a table, but scarcely felt the pain. She fumbled for the switch, found it, and flooded the room with light.

The clock on the wall announced three minutes had passed.

Chapter
Twenty-five

The channel to the Other Side opened and John drifted toward the light with agonizing slowness. Like the undertow of the ocean, Karyn's emotions tugged at him, threatening to drag him back. He fought the pull, twisted away, and closed his mind to her frantic appeal.

He couldn't be distracted. Time was running out.

He hoped Sandy knew he was trying to contact her. He'd never had trouble before reaching people he needed to contact, but he had no idea how it worked, just that it did. And there had never been such urgency before.

The tunnel behind him filled with mist, cutting him off from his earthly body, another buffer between him and the living world.

Sandeeeee. . . . he called. *Sandeeeee. . . ."*

"Go back." Mr. Boswell appeared.

"I have to find my sister . . . Help me, please."

Mr. Boswell emanated genuine regret. "I'm sorry. I can't do that. You shouldn't even be here . . . you must go back while there's still time. Your intention will be forgiven if you leave now."

"Not until I find my sister."

"John, please listen. Don't do this. You must not interfere with the way things are supposed to be. It's not too late. You still have time to reverse your path."

John turned a deaf ear to Mr. Boswell's plea. "Sandeeeee. . . ."

* * *

Karyn ran to the bed. With light restored, she could see he wasn't breathing. Why had she waited so long? She hadn't believed he could die.

She spotted a stethoscope on the table, put it on and held it to his chest, listening for a heartbeat, signs of even shallow respiration.

Nothing.

Karyn ripped off the stethoscope, ran to the door, and fumbled with the lock.

"Help! Somebody help!" she cried in the empty hall.

She froze with indecision.

Should she start CPR or go for help?

What if she ran for help and by the time she found someone, it was too late? She'd already lost precious minutes. The realization propelled her into action.

Karyn ran to the bed. She tilted John's head back, cleared his throat and placed her mouth over his.

* * *

John wandered through the mist, calling for his sister. Rather than providing clarity as it usually did, the mist closed about him, hindering his progress, walling him off from the souls on the Other Side. He couldn't reach anybody. Even Mr. Boswell had faded away. All he felt was emptiness. A void.

Alone.

He was completely alone.

Where had everyone gone?

Sandeee. . . . The peace he usually found here disappeared, replaced with anxiety and tension. Isolation. Why wouldn't someone help him? Where was his sister?

"We can't help you." His grandmother materialized. "It is against the Way. You know it is against the Way, and that's why you are having such difficulty."

"Where's Sandy?" John sent out a mental probe, trying to penetrate the fog.

"I know your pain, John. We all feel your pain. Please let her go. She chose the path that led her here. It is meant to be."

"I can't. What about Justin and Chelsea? Mom and Dad? They didn't choose this path."

"It is not for you to decide the path of others. Nor is it ours. That's why we cannot help you."

"Can't or won't?" he snapped.

"Is there a difference?" she asked calmly.

John tried a different track. "Look, just let me speak to her. Let me know that she is all right. I never got a chance to say good-bye."

"Why do you need to say good-bye, when you could visit her here?" His grandmother was aware of his ruse.

"It's not the same," he protested. "Grandma, Sandy has a *life*. Life! I don't buy it that this is what's meant to be. Fate is a path. You said so yourself."

"And this is where her path led. You're not supposed to change that John." She turned away and dissolved into the mist. "A soul in Limbo must make his or her own choice." Her words lingered.

She was gone. John wanted to weep with frustration.

It wasn't fair. If Sandy was in Limbo, he should have the right to influence her.

Limbo! That's where she was. And suddenly he

knew what everyone was hiding. There *was* still time to change his sister's path. She hadn't yet made the final journey.

John concentrated his thoughts, focused on Limbo.

* * *

Karyn lifted her mouth from John's, traced his breastbone, found the tip, then moved up three fingers. Covering one hand with the other, she placed her palm on his sternum and began to thrust. "One, two, three," she counted aloud.

Only five minutes had lapsed since she had begun CPR but it seemed like forever. If she'd had time, she might have considered the irony. John's sister was in ICU being resuscitated by a team of medical professionals, and John was in a lounge being given CPR by a social worker whose sole training consisted of a weekend Red Cross CPR class. Karyn stopped thrusting and resumed breathing, pinching John's nose shut so that the air she exhaled would go into his lungs.

Come on, Goddamnit. Breathe! I believe you, okay? I believe you can die and return. Now, just show me the return part, she begged silently.

* * *

Arriving in Limbo, John located Sandy immediately.

And Reid.

"Sandy, come back, please," John beseeched.

"John? What are you doing here?" Sandy was surprised to see him.

"I came to bring you back," he said.

The mist quivered. "I don't want to go back," she said. "I want to go forward." Her soul seemed to smile at Reid.

"Not yet. It's not permanent. You could come back, if you want to. But you have to want to," John said.

"Grandma is here. Did you know that?" Sandy exuded wonderment. "Of course you know. You've been coming here for years. This is what you do! Oh my God. This is what you do! You come here. Like this."

"Sandy—" John began. "Time is running out, for both of us. If you don't decide now, the situation will be irrevocable."

"John, we're staying here," Reid spoke. "Here we can have a new beginning forever. It will be like it was in the beginning. Only better."

"Much better," Sandy agreed.

John could feel his sister and brother-in-law's souls twining around each other, and he knew he was fighting a losing battle.

The sentience of the Other Side gave them vision into Sandy's hospital room. Together they saw the nurses and doctors working. Felt their emotion. Uncertainty as to her survival. Their concern about brain damage if she did survive.

"I may not fully recover if I go back," Sandy said. "The life I had may be no more."

"Sandy, you can do it. Trust me," John pleaded. "It's not your time. You have to realize that. Justin and Chelsea need you. Do you want both your children to grow up without either their mother or their father?"

With those words, he sensed a weakening, not from Sandy, but from Reid.

"No!" his sister sensed it, too. "I won't go. Not without you!"

"Sandy, I can't go with you," Reid said. "It's too late for me. I've made the final journey. We still have forever. We'll be together, again. But Justin and Chelsea need you now."

Sandy tottered on the brink of decision. "This is my Way. This is my Path."

"Sandy, please," John begged. "Choose life. For yourself and your children."

"You have the choice," Reid said. "But I think he's right."

"You'll wait for me?"

"Forever."

* * *

Ten minutes. Her strength waned as fatigue threatened, but she pushed on. John still showed no sign of rousing, his lips bearing a trace of blue indicative of a lack of oxygen. He was dying—was dead—and she couldn't bring him back.

A man in a white coat barreled through the door and stopped short. "What's going on here?"

"Thank God," Karyn looked up. "Help me! He's dead. He's not breathing and . . ."

"Get out of the way," the doctor ordered, quickly checking John's breathing. "Go get help!" he said, as he took over CPR.

Karyn ran, stumbling on her high heels. The nurse's station was deserted. "Help! Help! " she cried, continuing down the hall, past patient rooms. A few of the ambulatory ones staggered to the doorway, watching with surprise. Finally a nurse did appear, rounding the corner with a stack of charts. Karyn ran to her, gasping for breath. She grabbed the nurse's arm, knocked the charts to the floor. "I need help. My . . . my boyfriend is dead. The . . . the doctor is with him. He needs help!"

* * *

The change was nearly imperceptible, but it sent a shiver of awareness through John. He'd won! Elation filled him, filled the mist.

"I love you, Reid . . ." Sandy said, and then her soul disappeared from the mist. She'd gone back to life.

"Thank you," John said to Reid.

"Take care of her," Reid said. "If she remembers this, let her know I'll be waiting, that I love her more than anything."

"I will." John promised as Reid faded away. He felt curiously light and charged at the same time. It was a heady feeling.

"Grandma?" he called. "Are you there?"

"I'm here," she answered in a strange monotone.

"I won!" John's exuberance spilled over, creating a wake of emotion that rippled through the mist. "I won!" His heart danced. "Sandy went back."

Victory surged through him. He had turned onto a new path in his travels. Think of the things he could do! The changes he could make. The lives he could save! And Karyn would believe him and stand by him. She'd understand now. He foresaw a new purpose. How could he have considered giving up the Other Side? It made him whole. He was meant to come here—it wasn't a choice.

"Grandma?" he called again, realizing she was uncommonly silent.

"You know you're not supposed to change things," she said sadly. "It's not the Way."

"But, it's _good_! Sandy is going to live!"

"John—" she shook her head. "You've been

coming here, how many years, how many times? You still haven't learned."

He frowned. There was censure in her tone and something else. It seemed like . . . grief? Now, he was confused. "What's wrong?"

"You can't go back," she said sadly.

* * *

In the intensive care unit, one nurse respirated Sandy's still form, while another prepared an injection. Another pressed down with rhythmic thrusts on Sandy's sternum. "Come on, damn it," she said.

The heart monitor began to beep.

A nursing student, new to the ICU, cheered.

"Thank, God," the doctor prayed.

* * *

Tears streamed down Karyn's face as she watched the doctor and nurses work on John. His shirt was ripped open and they had him on the floor. Another nurse burst through the door, wheeling in a crash cart, bearing medical equipment used for CPR.

"What's he on?" a young resident asked Karyn.

"Nothing," she cried. "Nothing, I think. He was g-g-going to g-g-get his sister." She scrubbed at her eyes.

"When?"

"Just now. Five minutes ago. He just lay down. He died so he could rescue his sister," she said, oblivious to the incredulous looks of the medical team.

Chapter Twenty-six

"**I** can't go back?" John repeated his grandmother's words, struggling to comprehend the elusive meaning, which slipped like a will-o-the-wisp into the fog. "What does that mean?"

"You broke the rule . . ." she trailed off. "We tried to warn you."

A chill blew across his soul, a draught where warmth should have been. "What rule?" Then it dawned on him. "Time? Oh God, the time!" Panic griped him. "I have to go back!"

He called to the tunnel of light to lead him to his body. The mist condensed, coagulating thick and heavy, blocking his escape, forming a solid wall between him and his life. Between him and Karyn. He flailed against the mist, trying to fight his way out, but the mist enveloped him, drowning him, swallowing his entreaty.

His grandmother reached out to him. "Not that rule. Your girlfriend's CPR would have bought you time," she said. "You changed Sandy's fate. The path she and Reid chose was supposed to end here. Today."

John suddenly became aware that his consciousness had widened. His mind filled with mist, the sentience of everyone on the Other Side and beyond. He no longer heard just Mrs. Boswell, Mr. Boswell, Mrs. Pembroke's husband, Grandma. He heard everybody.

His life, as he had known it, flashed before him in full, glorious, high-speed Technicolor and he understood, everything. The direction he had taken became clear to him—why had he never been able to see it? It was right there in front of him, clearly marked.

The awareness brought an awe of such profound proportions, it was almost unbearable. He looked around and saw the world as it was—perfect in its imperfection. He felt the joy, the sorrow, the pain, the ecstasy, the anguish, and the relief. It was all there and he was a part of it all. It was such a gift, it made him want to cry, to shout.

And the knowledge! He couldn't begin to describe it: He felt like a blind man given the gift of sight. John eyed the world, and he was awed.

Sandy was going to be okay.

He knew it. He could *see* it!

He watched as she regained consciousness in the ICU, the nurse leaving to tell his parents and Karyn.

Karyn! Her efforts to save him snapped into view. Her pain, regret, guilt—for having disbelieved him—reached out like a physical presence and touched him; her anguish sliced at him. He ached to comfort her.

"I'm going back," he told his grandmother. "I'm sorry."

"No, I'm sorry, John. You don't have a choice anymore. You can't leave."

"I have to be with Karyn," he insisted.

"That's not a decision you can make anymore. When you changed Sandy's fate, you changed your own," she said.

"What is fate but a path one chooses? That's what you've always told me. Haven't we always had a choice? We may not like the choices we have, but we always have them. If that's true in life, it should be true on the Other Side," he argued.

"But you've made a choice. And one choice ends another. You can't be permitted to return, because you broke an inviolate rule."

"Isn't there anything you can do to help me?" John cried and felt his grandmother's answering sorrow. "I couldn't help it. This was my sister. I've never done this before. I wouldn't do it again."

"You surrendered to the desire. There's no guarantee that you wouldn't do it again. If you returned to your body, you would not be permitted to travel to the Other Side."

"I have to come here. This is what I am," John insisted. For the first time, he understood from the depth of his soul what it meant to be mortal. No, to be a prisoner, shackled and bound by his physical self, taunted by the freedom that existed on the other side of the cage.

And the desire to travel would remain. What would he do with a need unfulfilled? But if he stayed, he'd lose Karyn, his sister, his family, his life!

Karyn would grieve, but she'd recover and meet someone else. When she arrived at the Other Side, it wouldn't be him she would come to see, but someone else, someone she hadn't even met yet, who didn't know she existed. John watched as the future changed before eyes. He'd done this. He had caused it.

And with his new-found sentience he knew Karyn had been his fate. The one he was supposed to be with his entire life and beyond. How could he abandon one destiny for another? It was too much to ask. There had to be something else he could do. He looked to his grandmother for help, but she shook her head.

He could relinquish his link to the Other Side. Or he could give up his life and the woman he loved.

And he had to make the decision now.

Chapter Twenty-seven

John was thirty-six the second-to-last time he died. He returned into his body to find a respirator cupped over his face, a doctor pressing on his chest, the woman he loved sobbing, and his parents hovering nearby.

"Grandma says good-bye," he said to his parents as he reached for Karyn's hand.

Order Form

QTY.	Title	Price	Can. Price	Total
	The Messenger **Robin Valaitis Heflin**	**$11.95**	**$15.95** **CN**	
	Shipping and Handling Add $3.50 for orders in the US/Add $7.50 for Global Priority			
	Sales tax (WA state residents only, add 8.6%)			
	Total enclosed			

Telephone Orders:
Call **1-800-461-1931**
Have your VISA or
MasterCard ready.

INTL. Telephone Orders:
Toll free **1-877-250-5500**
Have your credit card ready.

Fax Orders:
425-672-8597
Fill out this order form and fax.

Postal Orders:
Hara Publishing
P.O. Box 19732
Seattle, WA 98109

E-mail Orders:
harapub@foxinternet.net

Method of Payment:

☐ Check or Money Order

☐ VISA

☐ MasterCard

Expiration Date: _____

Card #: _____

Signature: _____

Name _____
Address _____
City _____ State ____ Zip _____
Phone ( ) _____ Fax ( ) _____

Quantity discounts are available.
Call (425) 776-3390 for more information.
Thank you for your order!